MW01128271

HIS CONTROL

THE HUNTER BROTHERS BOOK 2

M. S. PARKER

BELMONTE PUBLISHING, LLC

Copyright © 2018 Belmonte Publishing LLC

Published by Belmonte Publishing LLC

ISBN-13: 978-1986906395

ISBN-10: 1986906396

READING ORDER

Thank you so much for reading His Control, the second book in the Hunter Brothers series. All books in the series can be read stand-alone, but if you'd like to read the complete series, I recommend reading them in this order:

PROLOGUE

Manfred

I wasn't sure which was worse, watching my beloved Olive standing by the portraits of our son, daughter-in-law, and granddaughter while sobs shook her frail shoulders, or seeing my grandsons standing next to her, each face heart-breakingly stoic. All except for Blake. He'd been furious with the world from the moment he'd woken up in the hospital, and nothing Olive or I had been able to do had changed that.

A part of me still felt like this was all some horrible nightmare, that I'd wake up and find my wife sleeping peacefully next to me. She'd tell me that none of it was true, that Chester and Abigail were safe at home with Aimee and the boys. I'd go back to sleep, making plans to see them all soon so I could put this terrible dream to rest.

Except, only the real world could hurt this much.

And it couldn't be a nightmare because that would've meant I'd been able to sleep. In the past few days, I'd barely managed twenty or thirty minutes a night. Every time I closed my eyes, I was back in the hospital, standing next to my son's bed, listening to the doctor tell me that he'd never wake up, that I had to decide if I wanted to keep his body alive, or let him go. Or I was in the morgue, identifying Abigail and Aimee, both barely recognizable.

As awful as that had been, the worst moment was when I had to tell the boys. Blake was only four. He didn't really understand what it meant that his parents and sister were gone. For him, I didn't think it had sunk in that they would never return. Slade was only a year older, but he was starting to put things together. When I tried to leave the house yesterday to come here and deal with the paperwork that inevitably came with death, he wrapped his arms around my leg and begged me not to leave. When Jax had come over to get him, Slade had started screaming that if I left, I'd never come back.

I watched Jax now as he leaned over to Slade and fixed his brother's tie. He'd been helping with his brothers, most of the time without even being asked. I hated seeing such a weight on his little shoulders, but I didn't know how to tell him it was okay to just be a kid. I'd never been someone who'd expressed emotions easily. Olive had always been best at that, and Chester had been like her.

I was just grateful that I wasn't doing this alone.

"Mr. Hunter." Officer March drew my attention away from the boys. "If I could have a moment of your time."

I shook his hand, then motioned for him to follow me away from the long line of people still waiting to offer their condolences. Chester and Abigail had been well-liked, and everyone had loved Aimee.

"I'm sorry to approach you like this," he said, pitching his voice low enough that no one else could hear. "But I've been ordered to close the case and stay away from you."

It took a moment for his words to process. "What, exactly, do you mean?"

Officer March scratched the back of his head, his eyes darting around as if he was still worried about someone over-hearing us. "My partner wasn't too keen on me telling you that I thought what happened was no accident."

"I remember," I said, "but I believed you would be investigating anyway."

He nodded. "I was; and I *did,* actually. I visited the crash site again. Looked over the autopsy reports. Something was off, but I was still trying to figure it out when my captain called me into his office and told me that I needed to stop stepping on the detectives' toes." Another furtive look around. "The thing is, I spoke with the detectives yesterday, and they told me that they were getting ready to sign off on the accident report. My asking questions apparently made it look like they weren't doing their jobs." He looked away and then back again. "Or, at least that's what my boss said."

"You don't think that's the case?"

"I think someone doesn't want anyone looking too closely at what happened."

I shifted on my feet, my mind racing. I'd been going over this in my head every moment that hadn't been consumed with planning and business. A true accident – black ice, an animal crossing the road – would be awful, but the idea that someone had done this on purpose...it was unimaginable. What sort of person could put a plan into motion that would not only leave a family without their father, but almost guaranteed collateral damage? I knew that Chester's investigative journalism had created enemies, but I doubted any of them had the impudence to take a life.

Still, despite all those doubts, my gut said there was more to what happened than most people were seeing. I hadn't managed a multi-billion-dollar business from the time I was twenty relying only on visible logic. I'd always had good intuition, and now it was telling me that something smelled fishy.

But I was still going to be smart about it.

"What makes you think that you can't take the request from your captain at face value?" I knew Captain Hartman, and he was usually a straight-shooter.

"Because the order about staying out of the case wasn't all he said." Officer March leaned closer. "He told me to stay away from you specifically, that you didn't want me poking around in things."

My stomach sank. I hadn't spoken to Hartman about Officer March. In fact, the only conversation we'd had since the crash had been when Hartman had said *It's a hell of a thing, losing members of your family like that.*

Idiot.

"You're right," I said. "Something isn't right about it."

"If I keep looking into this, it could be my job," he said. His eyes were wide. "What do you want me to do?"

I scrubbed a hand across my chin.

"Grandfather." A tug on my sleeve made me look down as much as Cai's quiet voice. His little face was solemn, bright blue eyes clear. "May I be excused?"

I swallowed hard against the lump in my throat and nodded. Cai didn't run off. He walked, calmly and like he knew exactly where he was going and why. It wasn't a seven-year-olds way of doing things, but Cai had never been a normal child. Out of all my grandchildren, he was the one who reminded me the most of myself. Focused and serious, never showing how he felt about anything. Not even after losing three members of his family.

"How are they?" Officer March asked. "I mean, I know they aren't fine, not after what happened, but...dammit. You know what I mean."

I nodded. I did know. "They're as good as can be expected."

Cai disappeared around the corner, and I found myself wondering where he was going, and if I might join him. Cai had asked if he could go back to school this week, and I understood the sentiment. It had been difficult this week not to throw myself into work and escape that way.

"Mr. Hunter," Officer March spoke again. "What would you like me to do?"

I didn't look at him as I answered, "I don't want you to lose your job."

I heard his sigh of relief over the chatter around me.

"I'd hoped you'd understand." His hand touched my arm, and I turned to see him holding out a piece of paper. "I took the liberty of writing down the name and contact information of a private investigator I know. He's a good guy. Knows his shi-stuff, and he's discreet."

I glanced down at the paper before putting it in my pocket.

Bartholomew Constantine.

After all of this was done, I'd give him a call, see if he could find anything.

If there was anything worth finding.

ONE

CAI

Twenty-Four Years Later

I SHOVED MY CARRY-ON INTO THE OVERHEAD BIN AND wondered if I'd made a mistake in not asking my brother if the company plane could fly me back to Atlanta. I wouldn't have asked him to arrange a private plane again, not when it wasn't an emergency, but the company plane belonged to Hunter Enterprises, and since part of my trip had been spent dealing with issues related to the business, I could've justified it to myself.

Who was I kidding?

No, I couldn't have.

I felt guilty even thinking about the meeting with Germaine Klaveno, Grandfather's attorney, as business. It had pertained to the company, but only because the inheritance of Grandfather's shares – as well as the rest of the estate – were dependent on a few things.

Like my brothers and I reconciling our differences.

I folded myself into the window seat and mentally cursed myself for not being willing to wait one more day for an aisle seat. Coach seats weren't made with a six-feet, five-inch frame in mind, but I couldn't justify the expense of a first-class seat for a two-and-a-half-hour flight. Not when my money could be better spent elsewhere. The clinic where I volunteered was always short on funding. The cost differential between a coach ticket and a first-class ticket could mean the difference between the clinic getting an X-ray machine that worked and continuing to make do with one that gave fuzzy exposures half the time.

"That doesn't look very comfortable."

The woman looking down at me had tight gray curls, a blue cardigan, and those glasses with a chain that hung around her neck. Even though she looked nothing like my Grandma Olive, she had the same sort of caring, sweet air about her, and my throat closed up with the sudden memory.

She sat down in the aisle seat but stayed perched on the edge. "You know, whenever I fly out to see my son, I always buy an extra seat for my Sherlock."

I gave her a tight smile. It didn't matter if Sherlock was a dog or a cat, I'd be polite and not complain, even when I started sneezing.

"Except I had to put him down a few months back, and when I bought my tickets, I plum forgot that I only needed one."

Where was she going with this? It took all my patience to bite my tongue and wait for her to get to the point. Usually, I had extraordinary patience, but after spending this past week with my brothers, it was wearing thin.

"You see, what I'm wondering is if you wouldn't mind switching seats with me." She gave me that grandmotherly smile again. "I think if I was by a window, I wouldn't be thinking about my poor Sherlock. You'd be doing me a favor, sitting out here on the aisle, with an empty seat between us."

I nodded, unable to speak just yet. I couldn't remember the last time someone had done something kind for me without any thought of what they could receive in return. She might be saying that I was doing her a favor, but we both knew who was helping who.

When we were all settled in our new seats, I looked over at her. "Thank you."

She reached over and patted my arm. "Don't mention it, dearie. You looked like you've been having a rough time of it lately."

She had no idea.

I knew Grandfather had done the best he could, raising us boys. Grandma Olive had made things easier, but she passed only four years after my parents and sister, another blow to our already fragile family. Instead of everything we'd been through bringing us together, it had pushed us apart, each for our own reasons. But it didn't mean his death hurt any less.

"Pardon me."

I looked up as a flight attendant leaned over me to put something in the overhead compartment. She was pretty, probably a few years younger than me, and smiling down at me in a way I easily recognized. I didn't have the money that Jax and Blake possessed, or Slade's charm, but I wasn't hurting for it either, which usually made things worse when it came to women. Between my looks – a fluke of genetics – and my job – which I'd worked my ass off to get – I wasn't hurting for female attention.

The flight attendant closed the compartment and shifted her position to allow a line of passengers to go by. The fact that it pressed her right up against my arm and shoulder wasn't intentional at all, I was certain. I resisted the urge to roll my eyes. I appreciated confident people but brazen wasn't an attractive quality, in my opinion.

"Is there anything I can get you?" she asked, her dark eyes making the invitation out to be more than the usual peanuts and sodas.

"No, thank you," I said politely as I picked up my book.

"Whatcha reading?" The attendant rubbed against my arm with all the subtlety of a cat in heat.

"*Infectious Disease Precautions and Protocols in Urban Environments*," I said lightly. "I'm on the chapter about quarantine in areas with rodent infestations."

Horror and disgust were almost immediately covered by a plastic smile as she hurried along, but I knew I wouldn't need to worry about her bothering me for anything other than her usual duties.

"Are you a doctor?"

I turned to my seatmate to find her watching me with an amused expression on her face.

"Yes," I said. "My specialty is infectious diseases."

"I'm going to go out on a limb here and assume that you work for the CDC." She reached into her bag and pulled out a piece of hard candy. "You could have just told her to leave you alone because you needed to concentrate on an important case."

I shrugged. "The truth seemed like a simpler and more logical deterrent than coming up with a story that might only pique her interest."

The older woman held out another piece of candy. I took it and popped the peppermint into my mouth.

"Were you in Boston for business or pleasure?" she asked.

"Neither," I answered honestly. "My grandfather died."

Her face softened, and she reached over to pat my hand. "I'm sorry to hear that, dearie."

I gave her a tight smile. "Thank you."

The voice of the head flight attendant came over the intercom just then, interrupting any further attempt at a conversation for the moment. I leaned my head back and closed my eyes. I'd flown enough to know the speech given at the beginning of every flight. If I could clear my mind for a few minutes, I could be asleep before take-off and wouldn't wake up until we started our descent.

Except I couldn't clear my mind, and it wasn't the fault of the flirting flight attendant, or the kind, older woman. For once, it wasn't even my work that had my head buzzing.

No, it was those infernal requirements Grandfather had put on the distribution of his estate. My brothers and I had known that going our own ways was in everyone's best interests, and Grandfather hadn't said a word to the contrary. Why had he decided that, after his death, we should suddenly come together as a family?

We hadn't been a true family for nearly twenty-five years.

TWO

ADDISON

I'D BEEN ON THE PLANE FOR TWO HOURS, AND WE WERE getting ready to start our descent into the Atlanta airport, but I still didn't feel like any of this was real yet.

I applied for the CDC internship without any real hope of getting it. The University of Minnesota was good, but it didn't have a prestigious, ivy league name that opened doors. I finished my classes at the end of the fall semester, but I was still working on my thesis. My advisor had spoken to someone at the CDC and gotten my application for the internship moved to the head of the pile. Apparently, they liked what they saw, because, after just a single phone interview, I was on my way. It was the perfect work to do while I completed my thesis.

If I ever finished the damn thing.

No, I refused to think about how I'd been stuck for weeks. I was going to think positive. Like how getting to meet one of the premier scientists in my field would start my career off on the right foot. Or how I was going to be doing the most important work in my life. Or how this internship could possibly lead to an actual job with the CDC after I finished my thesis.

Or how I was *positively* certain that I was going to be one of those people who never finished their thesis and became a failure, doomed to return to their tiny hometown and bag groceries for the rest of their life before going home to their four cats and two English bulldogs name Frumpy and Grumpy and–

"Miss, please put your seatbelt on."

I looked up to see one of those obnoxiously polite smiles that professionals put on whenever someone's pissed them off. Apparently, I was the one hold-out on the seatbelt thing.

"Sorry," I muttered as I buckled it.

"You looked like you were about to pee your pants."

This profound statement was followed by the sort of high-pitched giggling that would've been appropriate coming from a child or some nattering teenager. My seatmates, however, were well past their childhood, and at least a decade and a half from anything resembling a teenager. Easily past thirty, both were wearing leopard print-halter tops and tight pants that would've been tacky even on someone the right age. Their makeup was caked on, but if anything, it made the lines etched into their faces stand out even more.

I wasn't a shallow or vain person. I was a woman of science. I understood that the way a person was put together was due to genetic programming, with some environmental factors thrown in for good measure. For example, I had the sort of orange-red curls that could be seen for a mile, and I had a long line of maternal ancestors to thank for them, as well as the freckles. My pale green eyes came from a great-aunt on my dad's side. My nose was my father's.

I liked to think I didn't judge others by their appearance, but it wasn't easy when people went so far out of their way to change the way they looked that it was difficult to take them seriously. To top it all off, the two women in the middle and window seats had been talking about me from the moment I sat down and hadn't even bothered to pretend they weren't. I had a lot of practice ignoring assholes, but those two were getting on my last nerve.

Still, I didn't even give them a glance. I had enough on my mind at this moment.

I pulled a folded piece of paper from my pocket and opened it. I had an eidetic memory, but I liked to write things down and look at them. They helped me focus. I also liked to make lists of things that I had to do and run through them over and over. I found it...soothing. Okay, so maybe it was a little OCD, but it had always kept my anxiety under control.

And moving to a completely different part of the country without knowing a single person was certainly anxiety provoking material.

The internship was for a year, which meant too long for a hotel stay, and limited the amount of time I could sign a lease for. Since I'd lived at home during college, I didn't have any furniture outside of my bedroom stuff, and all of that was falling apart.

The only logical choice had been to find a roommate. It'd taken almost the entire two weeks I'd had to prepare to find her, but I thought we were going to get along well. Her name was Dorly Mitich, and she hadn't once said that we were going to be like sisters.

I already had sisters. I didn't want another one.

The airport was huge, and I saw a lot of people staring around, looking like they didn't know where they were going, but I went straight for the map. I didn't understand people who didn't use maps or ask for directions. Too much time wasted.

Dorly's apartment was already furnished, which meant my two suitcases were all I needed for now. The one thing I hadn't wanted to bring on the flight were my books, so they were being shipped later this week. Hopefully. I'd probably have to call one of my brothers to go over to the house and take the boxes to the post office since the chances of my mother or stepfather remembering were slim.

I didn't *technically* need them, since I could remember every single page, but I liked to have the references. Besides, I'd color-coded passages with various highlighters. Green for my thesis. Orange for things I believed I'd eventually disprove. Yellow for random bits of information I just found interesting.

I pulled up my GPS on my phone to look over the layout of the neighborhood. I didn't want to accidentally end up at the wrong building. That would be embarrassing.

"First time in Atlanta?" the cabbie asked as he settled into the driver's seat.

I blew out a breath. "It is."

"Where are you from?"

Great. He wanted to play twenty questions. I gave him a tight smile. "Minnesota."

A half-hour later, I was standing in front of apartment 7B, wondering what I'd gotten myself into. A simple taxi ride had been enough to convince me that Georgia and Minnesota were worlds apart. And the accent? I could barely understand a word.

Still, I knocked on the door, because staying here was a necessary part of me getting to work at the CDC, and there was no way in hell I was giving that up.

Especially when it meant that I just might get to meet Cai Hunter.

I'd hung his articles on my bedroom walls as a teenager, treasuring each rare picture. He was gorgeous, but it wasn't his body that had me staring at him every night before I went to sleep. It was his brain. He was brilliant; and he didn't use that brilliance to become the sort of doctor that would make six figures. He used it to try to make the world a better place.

The door opened, and my new roommate stood in front of me. At five and a half feet tall, I wasn't always able to look women in the eye, but Dorly Mitich was only about an inch taller than me.

And that was where any similarity ended.

Short, spiky dark red hair that I couldn't quite tell if it was natural or dyed. An athletic build that made me wonder how much she worked out. And piercings. A lot of piercings. Eyebrow, lip, and earrings that ran from her earlobe all the way up and around the top. Thanks to the tank top she wore, I could see the tattoos that ran over both arms, her shoulders, and across her cleavage.

"Addison Kilar." She made it a statement rather than a question.

I smiled, liking her directness. "That's me."

She stepped aside and waved me in. "Come on. Let me show you around."

I stepped past her and set my suitcases next to the door. It was small, but not claustrophobic. The furniture was mismatched but had a funky, artistic vibe that my oldest niece, Pattie, would have loved.

"Kitchen to the right. Living room to the left. I never needed a table to eat at, but if you want one, we can look into going halves." Dorly headed for a short hallway directly across from the door. "Bathroom is the first door on the right. Closet is the second. My room's right across from the bathroom, yours is here at the end." She pushed open the door and stepped back to let me see inside.

It was about the same size as my room back home. The bed was a queen, which was nice. The dresser was battered but big enough to hold what I'd brought. The best thing was the space against the far wall where I could put a bookshelf at some point.

"This is great," I said, meaning it.

"All right. Let's go get your stuff."

"Thanks," I said quickly. "But I've got it."

She raised an eyebrow. "Those two suitcases? That's all?"

"My mom is supposed to send my books later."

"Books?" Dorly stared at me for a moment, then burst into laughter. "You're shitting me, right? You brought two suitcases, and your mom's shipping books."

"Yes?" I wasn't sure what was so funny, but it didn't feel like she was making fun of me.

Dorly clapped a hand down on my shoulder and gave it a friendly squeeze. "I think we're going to get along just fine."

THREE

CAI

THE FLIGHT HAD BEEN UNEVENTFUL, AND I'D GOTTEN through the airport in record time. My car was in the parking lot, right where Pansy said she'd leave it, and traffic had been minimal. I'd gotten back to my apartment a few hours ago, and I still hadn't been able to relax. I tried reading, pacing, exercising, and none of it worked. Nervous energy hummed through my body, and there was only one way I could think to get rid of it.

And I needed to be rid of it.

Before I left for Boston, I'd been close to a breakthrough for a new vaccine. My bosses had understood my need to go even though most employers only gave a day or two for the death of a grandparent, but I knew they'd be watching my progress closely. We hadn't even yet progressed to trials, but they expected a lot of me.

The golden boy.

Never took vacations, worked all hours, focused on a problem until it was solved.

And, most importantly, never cracked under pressure.

Which meant, every so often, I needed some release.

When I was first assigned to Atlanta, a woman I'd met for a

casual encounter suggested that we visit a club. I went along with her as it seemed the politest course of action. She hadn't liked what we found, and we hadn't stayed long, but a few nights later, I'd gone back alone.

Now, if I was feeling this sort of anxiety, this particular need for release, that was where I went. And, tonight was no different.

No, I thought as I paid the cabbie and walked toward the club. Tonight, *was* different because I now knew that Jax had similar predilections. My younger brothers and I hadn't exactly talked about it prior to our conversation with Jax, but one of the last times the four of us had been together, Slade mentioned the name of a club in Worchester, and both Blake and I recognized it.

Jax hadn't been in the room at the time, and we'd never had an actual conversation about it. It wasn't the sort of thing we talked about with each other. Except he had this time. He'd told all of us about how he'd gone to Club Privé in New York, which had been enough to shock all of us into a conversation about how it was becoming one of the premier BDSM clubs in the world. I was there just last year when a case had taken me to the Big Apple.

I still couldn't believe my buttoned-up businessman brother was into S&M. Slade and Blake made sense once I'd known. But Jax? I spent my entire life thinking I'd never measure up to him, and when I realized my sexual preferences weren't mainstream, I felt it was another way I'd failed. I'd spent so many years hiding my desires, and now hearing Jax was the same way had almost made me angry with him. As if it was his fault that I'd struggled with who I was.

I pushed those thoughts aside as I nodded to the bouncer and made my way inside. It was packed even though it was still early, and I scanned the crowd for someone who piqued my interest. I rarely lingered, and it was only now that I realized my reluctance to spend time here came from those feelings of guilt and shame.

Tonight, wasn't the night to explore that, however. I needed to get rid of this tension and focus on the work I'd be doing tomorrow.

A tall brunette walked past, and my eyes followed. As always, my brain analyzed everything about her, from her height to the asymmetrical shape of her hips, and then returned an approval. I crossed the room, barely even seeing anyone else in the crowd. I stepped into her personal space, and her head immediately dipped.

"Are you here with anyone?" I asked.

She shook her head, making her dark hair fall forward to cover her face.

"Would you like to be with me tonight?"

She nodded without any hesitation, which was good. I didn't like it when a sub was too tentative. Submissive was good. Timid wasn't my thing.

I looked toward the back of the club where the room information was displayed. It was still early enough that only one room was occupied. My preference would have been to take her to a hotel, but I couldn't bring myself to justify the cost for a single encounter that wouldn't take the whole night.

"Come." I held out my hand, and she put hers in it. Her fingers were long and slender, her skin warm.

The sign-in process was quick, with each of us giving only a single name and initialing the space regarding consent and safety. In only moments, we were heading for the second door.

Once inside, I ordered Lissa to strip, and she did so with an efficiency that pleased me. She was naked beneath her simple sheath dress, but her body was far from bare. Both of her nipples were pierced with small bars, and the right side of her ribcage was decorated with an elaborate rosebush, complete with bleeding roses. Her navel was also pierced, and a thin gold chain ran from the ring down between her legs where, I assumed, it attached to a piercing through her clit or labia.

"On your back on the bed," I ordered.

She complied without a word. I was beginning to wonder if she was able to speak at all.

"Play with yourself, but don't come."

She spread her legs, revealing hairless skin that was pink and glistening from her arousal. Her fingers dropped down, spreading her lips and showing me the gold hoop through her clit. Slender digits stroked the damp flesh at a leisurely pace, and I unzipped my pants. I moved closer, sliding my hand under my boxer-briefs to grasp my half-hard cock.

"Faster," I said. "But don't come without my permission."

Her fingers made small circles over her clit before slipping inside her body. Her movements remained smooth, a rhythm that said she'd done this, many times before, likely at the request of other men.

The thought didn't bother me. I would use protection, and we would go our separate ways. I could see her in another man's embrace as soon as we stepped back into the club, and it would only bother me if she had been left unsatisfied by the experience.

"Play with your nipple piercings," I said. "However you like them to be touched."

Her free hand went to her breast, squeezing once before flicking and twisting it. A moan escaped her lips, and her eyes flew open, seeking mine.

I nodded. "It's all right. You're allowed to make noise. Just no climaxing until I say."

She sighed, her expression almost frantic. Her hips were

starting to move, seeking additional pressure, and a fine red flush was moving across her chest. She was nearing orgasm.

I freed my erection, pushing my pants open enough for me to be comfortable but without hindering my movement. "Don't..." I warned.

Her gaze dropped to my cock, and her tongue darted out to wet her lips. As much as I enjoyed oral sex, I wasn't in the mood to give or receive. What I wanted was to have absolute control, and nothing accomplished that more than getting to decide when someone else climaxed.

Without taking my eyes off the fingers working her pussy, I took a condom from the pocket of my pants, removed it from the wrapper, and rolled the smooth latex over my cock.

I moved so that I was standing at the end of the bed, close enough to see how swollen and wet she was. I reached down and grabbed her ankles, pulling her toward me.

"Not until I say so," I reminded her.

She let out a whimper, and I dug my fingers into her hips. I lifted her, bending her body until my cock was right at her entrance and only her shoulders and head still touched the bed. I held her weight easily and saw no sign of discomfort on her face, save that of a woman desperate for relief.

I buried myself inside her with one thrust, and she screamed. Not one of pain, though I'm sure she was experiencing at least some discomfort as her body adjusted. No, that had been a sound of pure frustration.

An aphrodisiac to be sure.

I didn't draw it out, although another time I might have enjoyed torturing her a bit longer. At this moment, however, I was ready to find release. I used my arms as well as my hips, lifting her and pulling her back even as I rocked forward, driving myself deep with each stroke.

"I didn't tell you to stop," I said as I bottomed out for the third time.

She made a sound of protest but didn't argue as her fingers moved again, one set twisting and pulling her nipple until it was red and swollen, the other rubbing her clit in time to my thrusts.

Her muscles began to quiver beneath my palms and around my cock. I could see the strain on her face, but she still didn't stop or complain.

When she finally spoke, it was a single word, her voice cracking and breaking as she repeated it over and over. "Please, please, please, please."

Her body shook with the effort it took to hold back, and as the pressure in my balls tightened, I finally gave in.

"You may come."

She let out a wail, and her body convulsed, her pussy squeezing me so hard that my own orgasm had an edge of pain to it. I fell forward, releasing my grip on her as I caught myself on my hands. I held my body over hers, eyes closed as I enjoyed the nothingness that came with the pleasure.

Maybe I'd actually sleep tonight.

FOUR

ADDISON

I was going to throw up.

From the moment I received the call saying I'd been chosen for the internship, I'd been dealing with butterflies, and it hadn't gotten better. Then, yesterday, one of our neighbors brought over a letter that'd gotten into their mailbox by mistake. A letter from the CDC confirming my internship.

And telling me that I'd specifically been assigned to Cai Hunter.

That's when my stomach decided that it didn't want to hold anything ever again.

I scrubbed my palms on my thighs, hoping they'd stop sweating when I shook Dr. Hunter's hand. I was probably going to make a fool of myself anyway. I didn't want to add gross to strange.

I was ten minutes early and standing outside with the sun shining down on me was only making everything worse. With my luck, I'd end up with a sunburn to make me look like the gangly, freckle-faced, small-town geek I'd always been. I took a slow breath to steady myself, reminded myself that I'd prepared for this, and then went inside.

The place was huge, but I'd looked at every picture and layout I could get my hands on, so I knew exactly where I was going. I'd expected someone to be there waiting for me, but no one was, so I paced and tried to look like I knew what I was doing.

"Addison Kilar?"

I turned around to see the owner of the voice glowering at me. She was close to my height but carried some extra weight that her wardrobe hadn't been adapted for. She was probably in her early thirties but was trying to look younger. Her light brown hair was teased into some strange hairdo, and her mouth was painted bright red.

I processed all of this in just a few seconds, then smiled and walked over to her. "That's me."

She didn't smile back and gave such a cold look to my outstretched hand that I pulled it back in a hurry. "Well, I'm Ms. Kemyss, and you're late."

I frowned. "I thought I didn't start until eight o'clock."

She inhaled deeply, one of those deep sighs that mothers or teachers gave when they're irritated but are trying to not explode. She pointed at the clock on the wall. "It's five after."

I reached into my pocket and pulled out my phone. "I think your clock is fast." I smiled to lighten what she clearly took as a reprimand because the disapproval on her face grew. "We don't allow phones. You'll need to leave yours with security, and you can collect it at the end of the day."

That hadn't been mentioned in the online code of conduct and expectations, but I wasn't going to argue with her about it. She looked like the sort of woman who'd slap me if I dared question her.

"Oh, okay." I looked around for the security person I needed to give my phone to, but no one else was nearby. "I was told I'd be working with Dr. Hunter. I'm sure he has something he needs me to do."

A smile finally appeared, but it held no warmth. It was worse than the blank stare she'd been giving me. Damn. I thought people in the South were nice.

"I'll be telling you what you need to do." She eyed my clothes, a slow examination down to my shoes and back up to my hair. Her lips pressed together. "And I'll get you the employee handbook to read over."

This wasn't what I was expecting, but it was my first day in a new place, and it was a place I really wanted to be...which meant this wasn't the battle to fight.

I smiled, trying to warm her over to me. "Sure thing. Lead the way."

Less than an hour passed before I realized that Pansy Kemyss wasn't one of the doctors or scientists here. I didn't know what her actual title was, but she basically recorded information for the scientists. After taking me on a tour and introducing me to all the scientists – well, almost all, since I had yet to see Dr. Hunter – she then sent me to drop off my phone at the security desk, then go around and ask if anyone wanted coffee.

I was one thesis away from achieving my doctorate in infectious diseases while also working on a thesis about a link between genetics and infection.

And I was getting coffee.

But I ground my teeth together and worked to impress everyone by getting everyone's orders perfect without writing anything down. For all I knew, this was the sort of thing every new intern had to do, something to keep them humble. I could do that.

Besides, it was one day. Once I got my bearings I'd decide how to improve the situation.

"Hey, kid," Pansy called from her desk.

I bit my lip and didn't take the bait. Even if the activities were normal, my gut told me that the way Pansy was treating me was personal. I just didn't understand why. I'd never had someone take such an instant disliking to me, and the scientist in me was curious about the cause.

"Run these down to Dr. Lodge, then start taking lunch orders." She held out a stack of papers. "On Mondays, we usually order from the bodega down the street. If it's raining, there are extra umbrellas in the break room."

I took the papers and headed down to Dr. Lodge's office. I'd take the opportunity to introduce myself by more than just my name. Pansy hadn't told anyone that I was an intern working under Dr. Hunter, just that I was new.

Unfortunately, Dr. Lodge wasn't in his office, and I didn't want to waste time waiting for him. Lunch was a way to make a good impression, and breaking bread with someone was always good. Besides, I had time to show them all I could do.

My feet were hurting by the time I was done distributing everyone's meals, but I still smiled and scurried off when Pansy sent me to get yet another coffee. If the super-saccharine, double foam mocha shit she sent me out for could even be rightly called coffee.

As I hurried back, I reminded myself that it was better for my career to be getting coffee for someone at the CDC than it was to be sitting at home in Minneapolis, staring at the screen of my laptop and wishing that I didn't have insane writer's block.

Maybe I could use the time I was doing inane tasks to do some mental preparation. I had a specific gene sequence that was giving me some trouble. If I could just figure out...

My thought process was interrupted as I ran into something solid. And then it was interrupted even more as hot coffee exploded all over me...and all over the person I'd run into.

I tipped my head back and looked up, up, at one of the tallest men I'd seen. And gorgeous. Golden blond hair. Bright blue eyes.

Shit.

Cai Hunter.

I'd just spilled coffee all over Dr. Cai Hunter.

Fuck my life.

"I am so sorry." I grabbed tissues from the nearby desk and started trying to clean Dr. Hunter's jacket. "I can't believe I did that. I've been carrying coffee and food all day and haven't spilled a drop." I sighed, rubbing harder and muttering faster. "It's not like I can even blame not knowing where I was. I've already walked this same path ten times today, and I have a perfect memory, so I know every detail along the route. It was stupid. I was trying to think through my thesis, and it distracted me, and I just ruined your jacket—"

"Were you burned?"

His voice jolted me out of my babbling. "What?"

"You look like you got the worst of it." He gestured at me, his blue eyes filled with concern. "Did it burn you?"

I looked down.

"Shit on a shingle." A laugh burst out of Dr. Hunter and color flooded my cheeks. I swiped at my shirt with already soaked tissues. Unsurprisingly, it didn't do any good. "Sorry about cursing. It's just my first day, and I thought it was going to be this great experience, and I've been getting coffee and running errands, and I can't even get that right."

I needed to stop talking, but my mouth wasn't getting the message.

"At least Miss Kemyss likes it less than scalding. Otherwise, I'd be in pain right now instead of only wet and embarrassed, though maybe if I'd been burned, I'd feel less like an idiot."

"It's just coffee," he said.

I looked at him, wondering if maybe this awful experience could have something good come out of it.

And then I saw what *he* had been holding when I'd thoughtlessly run into him.

A beaker.

Which was now empty.

"Shit on a shingle!" I said again. This time, however, all the color drained from my face. "Did I just start the zombie apocalypse? Coffee introduced into what had been a stable environment causing a mutation that could end the world as we know it?"

Would someone please shut me up?

"Or maybe it didn't need to mutate. It could've been the kind of thing that was completely harmless when kept in an airtight container, but as soon as it was exposed to air, it became airborne and transmittable. I'm like that guy at the beginning of that book *The Stand* where he sees the virus is loose but runs like an idiot and ends up destroying the world when he should've been paying attention to what he was doing and maybe–"

"Hey, hey, it's okay." He reached out and touched my arm.

A jolt of electricity ran across my nerves, and my mind went blissfully blank.

FIVE

CAI

I'D LEFT MY LAB TO TAKE A WALK AND CLEAR MY HEAD. Getting laid last night had helped me sleep, but it hadn't done anything to help me focus on the problem I ran into this morning. That problem had been circling in my mind over and over, and all my walk had done was given me a rhythm to mull by.

Then I walked straight into someone who'd been paying as little attention as I'd been, and everything changed.

I stared at her as she talked, fascinated by the rapid-fire way she spoke, as if her thoughts were connecting on a level that her mouth couldn't quite keep up with. I knew how that felt. I rarely tried to articulate my ideas because I always seemed to be skipping things and then having to go back and re-explain, and that never went well. People always ended up being confused. I couldn't even really write them well. My brain worked great when it came to numbers and chemistry, but communication, not so much.

It was one of the reasons I didn't often have conversations with women. Simple commands were easier.

Normally, people who talked a lot bothered me. It seemed a waste of time using so many words when just a few would suffice, but I didn't get that impression from the pretty redhead. She was nervous, and the words were a result of that, as much a part of her unconscious response to stress as someone who tapped their toes or chewed their fingernails. The biggest difference was that her nervous tick revealed a lot about her, and I found it fascinated me.

Once she started rambling again, this time about zombies and ending the world, I was tempted to see how long she would go before she realized that no one else was panicking, but then I saw that she was truly distressed, and knew I couldn't do that to her.

"Hey, hey, it's okay." I touched her arm, and her head jerked up, eyes meeting mine.

I'd never seen eyes quite that shade of pale green before, and something about them quieted the chaos in my mind. Or maybe it wasn't her eyes as much as it was her. Whoever this young woman was, she managed to do what little else ever had.

She distracted me.

"I was cleaning some things in my lab," I said, my hand still on her arm. "The beaker just had some soapy water in it."

She gave me a strange look. "You were carrying a beaker of soapy water?"

I shrugged and gave her a half-smile. "I forgot I had it, honestly."

She smiled, her cheeks flushing prettily. "I'm glad it wasn't some sort of flesh-eating virus that was going to turn us all into brain-munching zombies."

I laughed, wondering if it was me making her nervous enough to babble this time. I couldn't say the thought was a bad one. "I'm Cai Hunter."

She stared at me for a moment, like I'd said something strange. "I know who you are, Dr. Hunter. Anyone with an interest in infectious diseases or the cutting edge of science today knows who you are."

She looked down at my hand on her arm, and it was my turn to flush. I'd been moving my thumb over her skin without even realizing it. I had a moment to register how soft it was before dropping my hand. I didn't want her to get the wrong impression.

"You have me at a disadvantage," I said, hoping the change of topic would distract her from my momentary lapse of judgment. "You know my name, but I don't know yours."

"Addison Kilar." She held out her hand, then dropped it before I had a chance to shake it.

"And you work here?"

"Sort of."

She had an accent, I realized, and it wasn't a Southern one. I couldn't quite place it, but I'd heard it somewhere before.

"How does one 'sort of' work here?"

"I'm an intern," she said. "It's part of me finishing up my doctorate. Well, finishing up my thesis, more accurately. My advisor thought it'd look better if I was working here while writing rather than me not doing anything but still not able to finish the damn thing." She looked away and fidgeted with one of her curls. "I'm sorry, Dr. Hunter. Sometimes my mouth just runs away with me. I'll go get something to clean this up and then get another coffee for Miss Kemyss. You can give me a dry-cleaning bill, or I can pay for your shirt to be replaced. It was my fault for not watching where I was going."

"Nonsense," I said. "I wasn't paying attention either. It's as much my fault as yours."

She shook her head. "It's completely my fault. I was trying to work through some of my writer's block."

"You said you're working on your thesis?" I drew her attention away from blaming herself. "What's it about?"

"The link between genetics and infection." She looked down at herself, and then at me again. "Um...I think I should find something I can use to clean this up."

I shook my head, frowning. "You're an intern, not a janitor. And at the CDC, that is what's important. They have all sorts of guidelines they must follow and paperwork to fill out. In our labs, we have different procedures, but for public areas, we have to alert the janitorial staff and let them handle it."

Her eyes widened. "For coffee?"

"To make sure the spill was indeed coffee and soapy water, and *not* something that would turn us all into zombies or wipe out the world."

She looked as startled by my attempt to joke as I was.

"Okay. I'll tell them what happened."

"Have you eaten lunch yet?" The question burst out of my mouth, leaving me wondering if something had happened to my brain today to cause me to act so out of character with this stranger.

"No, I just got back from the lunch run." An expression of horror crossed her face. "I'm so sorry! Miss Kemyss didn't show me your office on my tour, and I completely spaced when I went around. I didn't even think about your lunch—"

Something didn't sound right. Why was an intern so close to finishing her doctoral thesis doing those sorts of errands? I needed to find out more information. Plus, it appeared she was working on something close to my own wheelhouse, and I wasn't arrogant enough to believe that I couldn't benefit from another person's perspective.

"I was just thinking about getting lunch," I said. "Would you join me? I'd like to discuss your thesis, and perhaps pick your brains about a problem I'm currently having."

Now she looked like she was going to throw up. Maybe lunch hadn't been a good suggestion after all.

Or maybe her stomach was twisting like mine, without explanation.

"That would...I mean...thank you, Dr. Hunter. I'll have to go ask Miss Kemyss, but I would be honored to have lunch with you."

"Pansy? Why do you need to ask her about lunch?" Pansy wouldn't have a doctorate student as an intern if she'd had an intern at all.

Her expression was puzzled. "She's my supervisor. I'll let her know I'll be going to lunch as soon as I..." she looked down and frowned, "do something with my shirt."

I managed not to scowl. I didn't want her to think I was mad at her. She hadn't done anything wrong. Pansy, however, I was going to have a word with. "Pansy isn't your supervisor. Interns at your level are assigned to specific doctors. You should have gotten a letter."

"I did," she admitted, chewing on her bottom lip. "It said I'd be working under you."

I'd heard enough. "I'll speak with Pansy and let her know that I'll be taking over your supervision from here on out. Do you have another shirt to change into?"

Addison shook her head. "I didn't think to bring one."

"That's always a good idea," I said. "Because if it's not coffee, it could be a contamination issue where all of your clothes have to be destroyed."

She stared at me. "Does that happen often?"

I thought for a moment. "Three times since I started working here, but all precautionary." I pulled my shirt away from my skin, only now just realizing how uncomfortable I was. "We keep a few extra items of clothing in the storage room down the hall and to the left, second door on the right. We just ask that anyone who has to take anything washes it and returns it; or replaces it with something new."

She nodded.

"I'm going to change as well, and then I'll meet you at the front doors in fifteen minutes. Will that be enough time for you?" She didn't appear to be one of those women who took forever to get ready but looks could be deceiving.

"Yes, that's plenty of time." She smiled, looking relieved. "Thank you, Dr. Hunter."

"Cai," I said, returning her smile. "There are some people here who love to hear the word *doctor* before their name, but I prefer Cai."

"I prefer Addison." The color that had faded from her cheeks rushed back. "For me, I mean. I prefer Addison to Miss Kilar."

"Now that we have that squared away, what do you say we take care of this mess and get some lunch?" I glanced toward the part of the corridor that would take me to Pansy's office. "I'll have Pansy call the janitors after I've cleared up this misunderstanding regarding your supervision."

As Addison hurried off, I sighed. Pansy and I had gone to college together, and I'd tutored her on and off while she'd worked on her master's degree in organic chemistry. Unfortunately, she hadn't been accepted into the doctorate program, but that hadn't stopped her from wanting to do some good in the world. She applied for a position at the CDC right after I was hired, and even though most of her job was compiling and recording data, it was important work.

Which was why I didn't understand her current behavior. If Addison had been an undergrad or hired as an assistant, running errands would have fallen in her purview, but an intern with Addison's qualifications should be working in a lab. I supposed it was possible that Addison hadn't felt comfortable telling Pansy that she'd been assigned to me, but Pansy knew how things worked. She should have asked immediately if Addison knew who she was working under.

I wasn't looking forward to reminding her that we had procedures for a reason. But, I told myself, it was better for me to talk to her about it rather than reporting her to HR. I understood that the rules and hierarchy existed for a reason, but in this case, I thought it wasn't worth all the hassle when a reminder would do.

Besides, filling out the paperwork would take a couple hours at least, and I'd rather spend the time talking to my new intern about her paper and my experiment. I couldn't wait to see what that brain of hers could do.

SIX
ADDISON

BREATHE.

Breathe.

Inhaling and exhaling was one of those things that people learned at birth, but I was twenty-two. I should know how to do this, but now, I was feeling fortunate to be able to put one foot in front of the other without making a fool out of myself. Again.

Cai Hunter.

I was going to lunch with Cai Hunter.

I had just told Cai Hunter about my thesis, and he sounded quite interested.

I'd also spilled coffee all over him and then babbled on about the most, inane things, including the damn zombie apocalypse.

I was mortified.

But I was also elated.

Because even though I'd made a complete ass of myself, he still wanted to talk to me.

Cai Hunter wanted to talk to *me*.

I kept repeating the sentence as I walked down the hall in search of the room with clean clothes. I kept repeating it as I changed, and as I went back to the front door, but I still couldn't believe it.

I'd been practically worshipping him since I was thirteen-years-old and first saw him on the cover of some science magazine at school. I'd followed his career ever since, digging for every bit of information I could find, but nothing could have prepared me for seeing him in the flesh.

And what magnificent flesh it was too. I wasn't the sort of woman who drooled over every cute guy, but Dr. Hunter – *Cai* – was far beyond cute. He was gorgeous.

As I approached I slowed my steps, so I could take him in, hoping that by the time I reached him, I would somehow be immune to whatever it was about him that turned me into a jabbering idiot.

"I see you found a nice shirt in our stash."

He gestured to the rather garish, long-sleeved yellow blouse I was now wearing.

"It was the only thing in my size," I said. "When you're all arms and legs, like me, clothes are a pain in the ass to find."

Shit. That hadn't been professional.

"I know the feeling," he said with a smile.

"Of course, you do," I said. "You're what, six-five?"

He nodded. "Good guess."

I didn't tell him that I'd read a profile on him three years ago. He'd think I was a stalker or something. If I told him I just had a good memory, he might think I was bragging.

I should've just kept my mouth shut.

"Looks like it's raining. Do you want to drive separately, or are you okay riding with me?"

"I don't know my way around," I admitted. "I just moved to Atlanta on Saturday."

"Then you'll ride with me." He started walking toward the parking garage. "Where are you from?"

"Minnesota."

It was strangely easy to talk to him, and the silence between us was comfortable too. The best part was that the whole car smelled like him too. Some sort of softly-scented soap and a hint of something more primal that I suspected was his natural scent.

As he drove us to our destination, he pointed out various parts of the city, much like a tour guide. But instead of giving me a history lesson or explaining the architecture, he always had some scientific bit of information. If I hadn't been able to see the sincere expression on his face, I would've thought he was making things up.

He surprised me as he pulled into a place called Amalfi Pizza. I'd had him pegged as a health nut, the sort of person who ate things like wheat grass and flaxseed. Gourmet pizza was not what I'd been thinking. My bank account probably wouldn't like this much, but it was just one meal.

And it was with Cai Hunter.

We were seated across from each other at a table small enough that my knees kept brushing his. We probably should've asked for a bigger table, but I was glad he hadn't. I knew this was one hundred percent work-related, but I planned on enjoying every minute of the one-on-one time I got to spend with him.

"You said that your thesis was about genetics and infection?" he asked after we gave the waiter our orders.

"Yes." I spread a napkin on my lap, fidgeting with the corner of the cloth. "I have this theory about how, if we better understood a link between genetics and infection, we could focus on correcting the genes rather than trying to eliminate the viruses. Gene therapy could be the new vaccine. Manipulate the genetic code in a baby, and they'd never get sick. Do it right, and they could pass the genes on to their descendants. It could eventually lead to an elimination of all illness. Of course, we'd have to factor in for mutations and a percentage of the population who either can't or won't consent to the gene therapy—"

My thought trailed off when I realized he was staring at me with something that looked a lot like fascination on his face.

"I'm sorry," he said with a half-smile. "I've just never heard anyone talk like that before."

Heat flooded my face, and I reached for my water, fingers bumping against the cold glass. I stopped myself before I knocked it over.

"Sorry," I muttered. "I tend to talk a lot when—"

"When you're nervous," he finished with a kind smile. "There's no need to be anxious. I believe that we'll work well together. I don't have interns working for me often because I have high intellectual standards. I won't send you out on pointless errands, but I will expect contributions. You've already proven that you see far-reaching effects rather than just an immediate resolution. From what I've seen so far, you have one of the most amazing minds I've ever encountered."

"I have?" The compliment made me catch my breath. I knew I was smart but hearing it from someone like him...it would've had me babbling again if the waiter hadn't come back with our drinks, breaking the moment.

And it was a good thing too, because whatever had been thickening the air between us hadn't been professional, and I needed us to be professional.

No matter how gorgeous he was.

SEVEN

CAI

I PEERED THROUGH THE LENS OF THE MICROSCOPE AND jotted down my findings on my notepad. Some of the other doctors liked to dictate their notes, but I'd never liked the sound of my own voice. Besides, it was a lot quicker to use the short-hand I created in college to take my own notes this way. My handwriting sucked, but I typed out my own notes, so no one complained about them.

"I finished transcribing your notes."

I jerked my head up. Addison had been here for five days now, and I still sometimes forgot she was here.

Except that wasn't entirely accurate. While my mind might've been focused on my work, some part of me was always aware of her presence. When she wasn't anxious she was quiet, which meant she could – and often did – show up at my side, startling me in the process.

I frowned, what she'd said finally registering. "What was that?"

She gave me a sheepish smile that I was starting to under-stand meant that she'd taken a bit of liberty with the freedom I gave her, but now she wasn't so sure whatever it was she'd done wouldn't get her into trouble.

"I finished transcribing your notes from this week," she repeated, her eyes darting around, landing on everything except me.

I turned around until I was facing her and crossed my arms, more curious than annoyed. Part of her contract included a non-disclosure agreement regarding anything she might see or hear during her internship, so I didn't need to worry about that.

"How did you do that?" I asked, studying her closely. "I created my own shorthand in college. No one else uses it because I've never told anyone else how to read it."

She reached up and tugged at a curl. "I might've cracked your code."

Now, I was intrigued. I stood up, grimacing at how stiff my legs were. I really should get up and stretch more often. "How did you manage that? I don't have a cipher written out anywhere."

She shuffled her feet, clasped her hands behind her back, and flicked a quick glance up at me.

Fuck.

She looked so submissive just then. Her posture, the way she dipped her head. All of it screamed at me to step into her personal space, to push back those sunset-curls, and tell her to tip her head back...

"I remember everything I see," she explained. "It can make my head really crowded. When I was a kid, I created my own sort of mental shorthand. Like compressing files on a computer. I can access them, when they aren't all pushing to the front."

"Interesting, but I don't understand how that translates into you figuring out in a week how to read something that I spent six months developing."

"In an interview with *Science Today*, you mentioned your

shorthand," she continued. "And there was a picture of something you'd written during the interview. When I was straightening your desk on Monday, I saw a few pages of your handwritten notes. On Tuesday, you had one of the transcribed files pulled up on your computer, and I saw it when I came up to ask you something. Once I had that in my head, connecting the dots wasn't difficult."

I crossed the space between us until barely a foot remained. "I knew you were brilliant from the first moment you started speaking, but this is beyond anything I could have predicted."

Her cheeks flushed, and I knew I'd embarrassed her. She deserved the compliment though. I'd done well academically, augmenting natural intelligence with hard work, but I didn't have a mind like hers.

"It was all your work," she said. "I mean, all I did was crack the code. You actually created it."

I reached out and hooked a finger under her chin, raising her face until she looked directly at me. "Don't sell yourself short."

The moment held, froze...and then shattered.

I dropped my hand and took a step back. What was it about this young woman that made me not only enjoy spending time in her presence but wanting to touch her? Innocent touches, like a brush of my fingers across her cheek, or putting my hand on her arm. I'd never been the sort of person who sought out physical contact, but with her, it was a fight to keep my hands to myself.

I didn't want to have sex with her. That would be far too cliché. The doctor sleeping with his intern. Even if it hadn't been cliché, I couldn't do it. She was even younger than I originally thought. Most people working on their doctorate were in their mid-twenties, but this child prodigy was only twenty-two. A college senior when she was just sixteen, she completed her graduate degree in only eighteen months before plowing through her doctoral program in near record time.

Twenty-two. Damn.

Too young for me.

Even though I knew there were plenty of couples with that age gap or more.

Not that I was looking to be part of a couple.

Shit.

I turned away, shuffling things on my table even though I had no real need. My thoughts had simply taken a train of thought too far. It happened sometimes. I'd be thinking about the way an epidemic spread, and instead of mentally picturing a week of an exponential spread, I'd have the whole mathematical equation worked out until the entire country was infected.

I'd learned to rein in those trails that served only to distract me. I could do the same now with my thoughts about Addison. Because that's all they were, a distraction from the real work here.

"Are you getting settled in?" I asked, the question practically bursting out of me.

"I am." Her voice was nice and even, like she hadn't noticed anything odd about my behavior. "My roommate is great. I'll admit, I was nervous about living with someone I'd never met, but we get along really well."

"How are your parents adjusting to your move?"

Why did I keep asking her personal questions? They weren't overtly personal, I knew, but they weren't helping my mind pack away the distractions. I should've stuck with discussions about viruses and anti-virals and cluster outbreaks.

Still, I waited for her answer, more curious than I wanted to admit.

"Well, I haven't spoken to my dad in a year, and before that, there'd only been calls on Christmas and birthdays, if he remembered."

I glanced over at her, but she was checking a few cultures I had growing.

"My mom didn't want me to leave, of course, but I think part of it was that she didn't want to lose her free babysitter." She said the words without rancor, but I heard a trace of sadness beneath them.

I turned around, then told myself that I didn't need to comfort her. I *shouldn't* comfort her. I was her supervisor, not her friend. Certainly not anything else.

"Sorry," she said, giving me a grim smile. "I love my family, but I don't always like them very much."

The admission made me chuckle.

She gave me a questioning look. "That's funny?"

"It is. Trust me, if you met my brothers, you'd be laughing too."

"Why's that?"

Now, she was the one asking personal questions. I needed to put a stop to this.

"I have three of them," I said, avoiding her question. "One older, and two younger."

"Do they still live in Boston?"

I raised an eyebrow.

She tapped her temple with her index finger. "Eidetic memory, remember? There's more than one article about you where it's mentioned that you grew up in Boston."

"My older brother, Jax, does. Slade lives in Texas, and Blake lives in Wyoming."

"Is it hard, being away from them?" she asked. "My sisters and brothers could be a pain in my ass, but I love them, you know?"

"My brothers and I...we get along better the farther we are apart."

She came over to stand near me, her head cocked to one side like she was trying to figure me out. "When was the last time you saw them?"

"Last week," I said, my jaw tightening at the memory. "Our grandfather died."

She reached out this time and put her hand on my arm. "I'm so sorry. I remember reading that he'd raised you after your parents passed."

"He did." I didn't shake off her hand even though the logical part of my brain told me to shut this down. Now.

She squeezed my arm. "It's never easy to lose someone."

I nodded but didn't say anything else. I didn't like this, talking about my family, about my feelings. I couldn't think straight when things were like this. I needed to take control again, get things back to the way they had been. I'd barely spoken to Grandfather in three years. The fact that he was no longer here for me to call or visit shouldn't have bothered me. He'd been no part of my life here in Atlanta, so now that I was back, things should've been able to go back to normal.

Except, now, as I looked at the concern on Addison's face, I began to wonder if my life would ever be normal again.

EIGHT
ADDISON

THINGS HAD GOTTEN, UM, STRANGE AT WORK TODAY. NOT uncomfortable or inappropriate, I didn't think. The things we'd talked about hadn't been anything I wouldn't have talked about with co-workers in the past. Okay, technically, he was my supervisor, but people talked to their bosses about things all the time.

Except I wasn't sure that the same questions would've *felt* the same with someone else. I wasn't the sort of person who talked about how things made me feel, but with Cai...I couldn't seem to separate my thoughts from my feelings around him.

Which meant I needed something to distract me.

Fortunately, the moment I walked into the apartment, I knew distraction was *exactly* what was going to happen.

Dorly sat on the sofa with her girlfriend, Codie Siko, but as soon as they saw me, both of their faces lit up in a way that made me second-guess my desire for distraction. I'd met Codie on Sunday, and I'd liked her as immediately as I had Dorly even though the two of them were as different as night and day. Where Dorly was blunt and didn't take shit from anyone, Codie was quiet and sweet, the type of person that automatically made others want to protect her. She had delicate features and a petite build, as well as a soft way of smiling that added to her fragile appearance.

It hadn't taken me long to realize that Codie wasn't a pushover though. She and Dorly balanced each other perfectly. If I'd wanted to be in a relationship, I'd want something like what they had.

But I didn't want romance or love or a commitment. Recently, I'd been thinking about the physical side of things more often, but I wasn't sure where to go with that, so I'd just left things where they were. Buying batteries for my vibrator was a whole lot cheaper than dating, and there'd never be a chance at hurt feelings.

"We're going out," Dorly announced. She gave me a once-over. "Go get changed."

"Where are we going?" I asked as I headed toward my bedroom.

"A club," she called after me.

"Shower first, then." I went into the bathroom instead. I wasn't expecting anything to happen, but I'd learned that it was better to be prepared and not need something than it was to be caught off-guard.

"Can I pick out your clothes?" Codie asked, raising her voice to be heard over the water.

"Sure." She had better fashion sense than I did anyway. I tended to find something I liked and stick with it for as long as possible. I thought about telling her I didn't want anything too revealing but decided it wasn't necessary. I didn't own anything that I wasn't comfortable wearing.

"WHAT THE HELL, CODIE?" I stared at the mirror, not recognizing the woman looking back at me.

She'd taken a lacy camisole top I'd gotten as part of a gift from Lottie and paired it with a plain white blouse, leaving the blouse mostly unbuttoned and tied off at the bottom so that it framed the low neckline and sheer material of the top. She'd vetoed a bra even though, if I looked hard enough, I was certain I could see the outline of my nipples.

Then there was the skirt. I had a suspicion that it had started life belonging to Codie. Or perhaps a child's doll. Either way, it fit me like a second skin and barely covered my ass.

"How am I supposed to bend over without flashing my underwear at everyone?"

Dorly shrugged. "The way I see it, you have two choices. Either don't bend over, or don't wear underwear."

I glared at her. I'd always had long legs, and this skirt made them look even longer. I'd at least won the right to choose my own shoes rather than a pair of five-inch heels that made me feel like the giant in *Jack and the Beanstalk*.

"We're not done yet," Codie informed me. She held up a small jar. "How do you feel about hair glitter?"

"I FEEL LIKE AN IDIOT," I muttered as I slunk along behind Codie and Dorly. "That's what I should have told her."

This was the last time I let Codie play dress up. On top of the clothes that were getting a hell of a lot of attention, she'd put some glittery gel shit in my hair, and now my hair was some brassy shade of bronze. And sparkling. So was my face thanks to the make-up Codie had put on.

At least one good thing would come from all this. If we ran into anyone from work, I doubted they'd recognize me.

The moment I walked into the club, however, I felt that the odds of me seeing anyone I knew had gone from slim to none.

Because this wasn't a regular club.

It was a sex club.

"Um, Dorly?"

She grinned at me. "Surprise."

I glared at her. "Are you kidding me?"

She gestured for me to follow her, then took Codie's hand so her girlfriend didn't get lost in the crowd. We tucked ourselves into a back corner where the music wasn't quite so overwhelming.

"I thought we were going to the club where you and Codie worked."

"We did," Codie said. "Dorly's a bouncer, and I'm a waitress. It's how we met."

"But this is a sex club."

Dorly half-shrugged. "Technically, it's a BDSM club, but most people don't make a distinction."

"The people here are really great," Codie said. "They screen everyone. You can't even walk in off the streets unless it's an open night. Everyone here is either an employee, a paid member, or the guest of a member."

Dorly nodded. "She's right. They take safe and consensual seriously. Complaints are investigated in-house with a team of badass security people, and they've got no problem calling the cops on someone if their behavior warrants it."

While still feeling strange about this being sprung on me, their reassurances helped with the anxiety. I'd only know them a short time, but I didn't believe they'd do anything to put my safety at risk.

"Everyone here's really open about sex," Dorly continued. "As long as you're respectful, you can ask anyone anything. They get all kinds. Gay, straight, bi. Masochists. Sadists. People with specific fetishes. Voyeurs. Exhibitionists. People in long-term relationships. Married couples. People just looking to hook up for one night."

"As long as it's safe and consensual, pretty much anything goes," Codie summed up.

I looked around again, letting my mind absorb everything at a slower rate now that the shock had worn off.

"I have to ask," I said after a moment, "why did you bring me here instead of a regular club?"

Dorly shrugged. "You looked like you needed to unwind, and what better way to blow off some steam than a good fuck? It's a hell of a lot safer to hook up with a guy here than it is to go home with some random from a bar."

"I don't think losing my virginity to a leather and whips stranger is really my thing."

Shit.

There I went, my nerves making my mouth run, and now I'd just blurted out that I was still a virgin, and I was getting that wide-eyed stare I hated.

Dorly gaped at me, and when she finally began speaking, it was a rush of words. "Shit, Addy, I'm sorry. I didn't know. I wouldn't have brought you here if–"

"It's okay." I said quickly. "It's not some religious thing, or me waiting for Mr. Right. I'm just the sort of person who likes to know what I'm getting into. I don't mean literally. I'm a scientist, so I know how sex works. There's no surprise for me there. Or unrealistic expectations. I know the average penis size and how different a male orgasm is from a female one. And it's not like I've never masturbated before–" I covered my face with my hands. "Someone please shoot me now."

Laughter made me raise my head, but Dorly and Codie didn't look like they were laughing *at* me, just at the fact that I couldn't stop talking.

"I'm sorry," Dorly said. "That was just a lot of information coming out all at once."

"I'm going to go home now." I started to stand, but Codie grabbed my arm.

"I think this is exactly where you need to be," she said. "You said you're not looking for love, right? You want someone who's going to come at sex from a logical point of view. Physical pleasure without emotional attachment. But you want someone you can trust to make sure you enjoy yourself, and trust not to be some sleazy stalker or someone dangerous."

"Right," I agreed. "I've been mentally and emotionally ready for years. I've just never had the time to figure out how to find someone like that."

Codie glanced at Dorly, then looked back at me. "I think I know someone."

"Who?" Dorly asked.

"There's this guy who comes in every couple of weeks or so. He's polite, respectful, and I've only ever heard good things about him. I don't know his name, because he's not much of a talker, but he's a member in good standing, which means his background check was crystal clean, and his behavior here has been above reproach."

"Who are you talking about?" Dorly asked again.

"We call him Mr. K," Codie said. "One of the girls heard him say his name once but couldn't hear it clearly. All she caught was the 'k' sound. First, last, we don't know that either."

"You know the important things, but not the personal things," I said slowly. Maybe Codie was right. Maybe this was what I needed after all.

"I can see if he's here tonight," Codie offered, "and ask if he's interested, and it can be as impersonal as you want it. From what I hear, that's exactly what he likes."

Tonight? I hadn't come here thinking about having sex for

the first time. Then again, I'd thought we were going to a dance club where I'd deal with the same sort of men I'd met back in Minnesota. I hadn't known we'd be coming here, or that a place like this could offer exactly what I was looking for.

There was one thing I had to make sure was clear if I was going to do this though.

"He'd need to agree not to do any of the whips and chains stuff," I said.

"Don't worry about that. That's part of the whole safe and consensual thing. You'll set down terms of what you want and what you don't want before he even touches you."

I nodded before I realized I was going to agree. "Okay," I said. "But if you're going to talk to him, I'd prefer if you told him up-front what I was comfortable doing."

Codie smiled. "All right. Let's start with bondage. How do you feel about handcuffs?"

NINE
CAI

TODAY HAD BEEN A WEIRD DAY. JUST ALL-AROUND STRANGE. I'd told Addison more about my family than I'd told any of my co-workers. In fact, Pansy was the only one who knew anything about my family, or anything personal about me, and that was mostly because we'd gone to college together. I'd spent so much time tutoring her that, inevitably, those sorts of things had just come up.

Maybe that's what'd happened with Addison. Outside of times when I was working with a team during an outbreak, I didn't spend extended amounts of time with anyone. It made sense that having someone in my lab would make me want to fill the silence.

Except that wasn't what happened. I hadn't been talking because things had felt awkward without either of us saying something. I'd talked to her because I'd wanted to. I wanted to know who she was, how her brain worked. She interested me.

Professionally.

I certainly didn't wonder what it would've been like to turn those platonic touches into something else. To feel her mouth under mine...

My dick gave an interested twitch.

That was just unfair. I'd been in the club for ten minutes, and a dozen half-naked women had walked by, but none of them had struck my fancy. It wasn't a physical thing. They were beautiful, sexy. I could see ways their features would be considered by many to be superior to...others.

"Hello."

A soft female voice caught my attention, and I looked around for a moment before looking down at a petite Asian woman I recognized. I'd talked to her a few times before. She was a waitress here, though I couldn't remember her name. I thought I remembered someone mentioning that she was dating one of the bouncers.

"I'm Codie." She stretched up on her toes, as if trying to make it easier to hear her. "Can I talk to you about something?"

I nodded and followed her a couple feet away to a shadowed corner. "How can I help you?"

She smiled in a way that made me wonder if I should've worded that differently.

"Have you found anyone to play with tonight?" she asked.

Dammit. Were my people skills really *that* bad?

"I thought you had a boyfriend."

"No," she gave me a shy smile, "a girlfriend."

She was dating Dorly, then, the only female bouncer in this place. But if Codie and Dorly were dating, then...

"I'm afraid I don't understand." Or, rather, I was hoping I didn't understand, because I really didn't want to have to break it to Codie that I didn't want a threesome with her and her girlfriend.

I didn't share well.

"Don't say no until you hear me out."

This was sounding better by the minute.

"I have a friend who's looking for a nice, anonymous encounter with someone who knows how to be in control."

I folded my arms. This wasn't getting any clearer. "What's the catch?"

"She's a virgin."

It was on the tip of my tongue to say *hell no*, and then go back to looking for someone to take to one of the back rooms. But something about Codie's request gave me pause.

"Why would she want to lose her virginity to a stranger at a BDSM club?"

"She wanted to feel safe," Codie explained. "But she also doesn't want a commitment. You know how it is, picking up someone at a club for casual sex." She gave me a probing look. "Or maybe you don't, being a large, strong man. But, for some of us, it can be...dangerous. Dorly and I told her that she'd be safe here."

"Then why me?"

She met my eyes. "Because I've seen you here. You're polite to everyone. Even though you're a Dom, you don't treat anyone like less. You don't go the humiliation or degradation routes. She needs someone who can take control and make her feel good, and everything I've heard about you says that you can do that for her."

Codie seemed genuine, and for once, I didn't want to be cynical about a person's intentions. Still, I had to ask.

"Did you tell her my name?"

She smiled. "I don't know your name."

Why wasn't I walking away?

Maybe because this was the first time since I left work that I hadn't been thinking about Addison.

"I would have conditions," I said. "No names. No personal details." I thought for a moment and then added, "I want masks. And no kissing."

"I'll talk to her, but I'm sure she'll be fine with that. She's not looking for anything beyond this one encounter." She gave me a quick list of some of the definite *don't*s, and then glanced toward the back of the club. "Next to the last door in the back. Be there in fifteen minutes."

It was the longest quarter hour of my life. I was torn between wanting time to hurry up and thinking I'd made a mistake. That little voice in the back of my head kept getting louder until I finally started walking toward the room Codie had pointed out.

She was waiting next to it, a mask in hand. "She agreed to everything."

I took the mask and put it on. "Thank you." As soon as the words were out of my mouth, I felt like an idiot, thanking her. Fortunately, she'd already gone back to her girlfriend and didn't see my cheeks growing hot.

I gave myself a few seconds to calm down and then went into the room.

The lighting was very dim, taking away the room's harsher angles. It took a moment for my eyes to adjust, and then I saw the figure on the bed. She was tall and slender, her face almost completely covered by a mask, her curls a glittery bronze that I assumed was some sort of coloring.

"Your friend said you agreed to my terms." I pitched my voice lower than normal, not wanting to frighten her. Domination didn't mean I needed to shout or scold. She was new to both sex and BDSM, which meant I needed to change my approach a bit.

"I did."

Her voice was soft, pitched so low I had to strain to hear. Like she was scared. Or maybe *she* didn't want to scare *me* away.

I was half-way through unbuttoning my shirt before I

remembered that I rarely undressed for sex. Then again, I was here primarily for her. I always made sure my partners left satisfied, but this was different. Being a Dom meant taking care of the needs of my sub. During the time we were in this room, she was my sub.

I finished taking off my shirt and set it aside. "You may call me 'Sir.' What would you like me to call you?"

She hesitated for a moment, then said in a voice that was very near a whisper. "May."

"Very good, May." I toed off my shoes. "I want you to listen carefully because I don't want there to be any misunderstandings. I'm going to explain how things will go tonight, and if you have any questions, please ask."

"All right."

For a moment, I thought she was going to say something else, but instead, she folded her hands in her lap and waited.

"The first and most important thing you need to remember is your safe word. Unless you have something else you'd rather use, I would like us to use one that I'm accustomed to hearing. *Watson*."

James D. Watson was a scientist whose work I admired, and his name wouldn't be something I'd likely hear in a sexual situation. Not that I'd ever had a woman know whose name it was. Most assumed it was either Sherlock Holmes' partner, or actress Emma Watson.

It didn't matter which one she thought I'd gotten my safe word from, as long as she didn't forget it.

TEN
ADDISON

I HADN'T REALLY THOUGHT ABOUT WHAT CODIE'S FRIEND would look like because I trusted her judgment about his abilities where it mattered. Then he'd come into the room, and my already churning stomach had done a flip. It'd been a good kind of flip because even though his face was covered, I saw enough to see that he was, well, *hot.*

And the fact that he reminded me of Cai both unsettled and comforted me at once. I knew, of course, that someone like him would never step a foot in a club like this but allowing myself to think it was him made my stomach twist with a desire I didn't want to think about.

It hadn't been easy to focus on what he was saying while he was undressing, but I'd managed, and now we were about to get down to the real reason we were here.

I laid on my back, trying not to start babbling like an idiot due to my anxiety skyrocketing through the roof.

"Relax."

No matter how quiet his voice was, that single word was a command, and it was as sexy as hell.

"Close your eyes, May."

I obeyed.

"What do you say if you want me to stop?"

"Watson," I said automatically.

"How are you to address me?"

A little thrill went through me. "Sir."

"Don't forget again."

"Yes, Sir."

The tip of a finger traced along my collarbone, and I shivered. My hands curled into the bedspread. If he could make me feel this way with that single touch...I was glad I wasn't adding emotions into things. I could only imagine what this would be like if I was doing this with someone I actually knew.

Then his lips touched my stomach, and my brain did something it'd never done before.

It stopped.

Oh, yeah, I could get used to this.

I made a soft, moaning sound and was rewarded with the sexiest chuckle I'd ever heard. I opened my eyes, watching as he kissed up my stomach, pushing my shirt up as he moved. When he lifted it over my breasts, I gave a nervous laugh.

"Don't doubt how beautiful you are," he said. "If you take nothing else from tonight, take this: never allow anyone to make you feel like you deserve anything less than a man who will adore you."

This wasn't like what I thought S&M would be like. Wet, hot lips and tongue licking and sucking every inch of my breasts before latching on to my nipple. I gave an inarticulate cry as pleasure shot straight south, making me press my legs together.

"Can I touch you?" My voice was breathless. The question seemed to startle him, and he raised his head. "You said I could ask questions."

He smiled, and I wanted so badly to see his eyes. "I did. Yes, you may touch me, but you're not allowed to touch yourself."

With hands and a mouth that talented, why would I even *want* to touch myself? I didn't ask though. Instead, I was touching all that beautiful, tanned skin and firm muscles. He wasn't huge but was just big enough for me to feel small, something most men couldn't do.

His teeth scraped over the tip of my nipple, and I dug my nails into his back.

"Are you okay?"

"Oh...yeah..." My eyes fluttered closed. "Again, please...Sir."

He did it again, and I squirmed. Teeth...good.

A hand moved down between my legs, and I spread them, eager for what new sensations he could offer me. He ran his finger along the damp crotch of my panties. They were the nicest ones I owned, and I was about to ask him to rip them off me because I needed him touching my skin.

"I'm going to take it easy," he said as he raised himself onto an elbow, so he could look down at me. "I'll do my best to keep you from discomfort, but sometimes, penetration for the first time–"

I shook my head, running my hand down his shoulder. "No need. I'm a virgin in the literal sense, but a medical exam might not agree with that assessment."

"Good to know."

He pushed up onto his knees and reached under my skirt. I raised my hips, watching as he slid my panties down my legs. I waited for him to finish undressing me, but instead, he returned his hand to where it had been before, this time, without anything between his palm and my pussy.

"I'm going to make you come," he growled. "And then I'm going to fuck you. And you're going to come again."

I shifted on the bed, desperately wanting to believe his promises, but too many facts were floating around in my head. The low probability of a climax during penetration. The number of women who experienced pain during their first time. The percentage of women who didn't even enjoy intercourse at all.

"May, look at me. *May*."

My eyes snapped up to meet his intense gaze, and I again wished I could see the exact color, but his eyes were too shadowed behind the mask.

"I will make you come." It wasn't a question. "And when I'm inside you, I'll make you come again. Trust me."

I nodded. "Yes, Sir," I whispered.

"Good answer."

He slipped a finger inside me, twisting as he moved it. The palm of his hand pressed against the top of my mound, pressure alternating until I gasped. He shifted, adding a second finger inside me, and his thumb slid between my folds to rub against my clit.

I'd used my own fingers, as well as a vibrator, but none of that compared to what he was doing to me. His thumb switched from back and forth movements to circles, and I grabbed his forearm.

"Yes!"

"There we are."

It wasn't until then that I realized he was reading my reactions, searching for the touch I needed to build the pressure inside me until I finally exploded. He wasn't a man who was simply using the same techniques he'd used on previous lovers, expecting me to respond to it. He was searching for what worked for me, as if all his focus was on my pleasure.

Wow.

"Come, little May. I can feel the tension in your body. You're close. Let go."

My nails must've been hurting him, but I couldn't seem to

get my fingers to let go. He didn't say a word about it as he continued to coax me toward orgasm.

Then, something inside me cracked, broke, and my back arched, muscles clenched, and I came.

When I was able to open my eyes again, I found him standing at the foot of the bed, his pants and underwear gone. I was still trying to process just how thick and long he was when I realized he was talking to me.

"I'm sorry, Sir." I propped myself up on my elbows. "I was...distracted."

His lips twitched into a smile for a moment. "Take off your clothes."

I sat up and pulled off both shirts I was wearing, then tugged off my skirt. I'd never been self-conscious about my body, firmly believing in health over a specifically desirable body type, but I was glad to feel his desire in the way he touched me, hear it in his groan of appreciation.

I licked my lips as he rolled on a condom, and I had a moment where I wanted to ask him to let me go down on him.

"Lie back down."

I didn't even hesitate. No matter how many facts I had in my head, I didn't doubt he'd be able to make me come again, and this time, it'd be with that mouth-watering piece of flesh inside me.

"Grab your legs behind your knees." The bed dipped down as he climbed on to it. "Pull your legs up and out. I want to watch my cock entering you."

I wanted to see that too, but I didn't argue. I'd already liked the idea of a man who knew what he was doing. I hadn't realized, however, just how freeing it would be to not have to think or decide anything. I could simply obey and feel.

"May, look at me. Are you certain this is what you want?"

No hesitation. "Yes, please."

Pressure, then a slow, aching stretching. My body accepting his, opening more with each inch. I no longer heard or saw anything. I was barely aware of my hands holding my legs. Nothing existed except the place where he was filling me up.

"Put your legs around my waist."

I hadn't realized I'd closed my eyes until I opened them again at his order. His voice was strained, and as I crossed my ankles at the small of his back, he put his hands on my hips, his fingers tense.

He rocked against me, rolled his hips, and then he eased himself out almost all the way before driving back into me. It took my breath away. And then he did it again.

With each stroke, a new ripple of pleasure washed over me, promising something bigger and stronger than before. I grabbed his hands, needing an anchor to keep me from floating away. He was solid and right there, holding me steady even as he pushed me toward the edge.

Neither of us spoke as I came again, but the deep, primal groan that accompanied the throbbing of his cock inside me was as good as my own name. I had made this amazing man feel that good. And there wouldn't be any repercussions, no awkward post-coital talk. We wouldn't need to worry about being uncomfortable if we saw each other somewhere.

Everything had been just as perfect as I could have ever wanted.

ELEVEN

CAI

I⊤ seemed that my intention to resolve my recent fascination with my intern by having sex with a stranger at a BDSM club had backfired on me. Now, I couldn't stop thinking about May unless I was talking to Addison. The whole weekend, that encounter kept replaying in my head. The way she'd taken to being submissive. How she'd responded to my touch. What it had felt like sinking into her tight, wet heat.

Usually, when I wanted sex, I found a partner, had sex, and then didn't think about the woman again. Not because I was an ass, but because it was never a specific *woman* I wanted. It was the physical pleasure, the mental break. Once that was done, she never crossed my mind again.

For some reason, that didn't seem to apply to the glitter-haired woman I'd been with Friday night. She kept popping into my head, and that wreaked havoc on anything I tried to do.

By the time I arrived at work on Monday, I was looking forward to anything that distracted me from *her*. When Addison came in, already talking about something completely off-subject, I was truly grateful.

"It's just surprising, you know, how much warmer it is here

than it is back home. I mean, it's one thing to know it on a cerebral level, but I go into a store and see Valentine's Day sales, and then walk outside in short sleeves and expect to be cold." Addison's cheeks were flushed as she put her purse into her desk drawer. "How long did it take you to get used to it?"

I allowed myself a smile before answering, "I honestly don't think I've ever noticed it."

"How can you not notice?" she asked, shaking her head. "I don't even want to think about being here for Christmas. I mean, don't get me wrong, I'm grateful to be here, and getting a permanent job at the CDC would be amazing, but I'd have a hard time getting into the Christmas spirit without snow."

"I don't miss driving in it," I said. "Though you'll want to be careful if you're ever on the road and it does snow. The whole city shuts down for something that Boston or Minneapolis wouldn't even blink at."

"Sounds like fun." She grinned. "There are five of us. Lottie, then Simon, me, and Gene grew up together. Erin and Angel didn't come along until later. The three of us older ones used to love the snow days when the snow was too high for even the plows to get through. I'm right between my two brothers agewise, and when it was too high for the plows to get through, Simon and Gene would dig out a tunnel, and we'd use it to get out of the house, so we could play. We'd have the whole neighborhood to ourselves."

"I'm sure Dr. Hunter has more important things to do than listen to stories about your childhood." Pansy breezed in with her usual smile.

Except the smile was only sent my way. As soon as she looked over at Addison, it fell away.

"Cai, Dr. Edison is asking if you had the time to review the paper he sent you?"

Shit. I hadn't been able to concentrate yesterday morning, so

I'd put the paper aside and I'd completely forgotten about it until just now.

"Not yet."

"Is it anything I can help with?" Addison asked.

Pansy made a derisive sound I'd never heard from her before. "You're an *intern*. Do you honestly think you'd be qualified to review a paper for one of our tenured doctors?"

What the hell was wrong with her today?

Addison's cheeks were red, and I could see sparks of anger in her eyes, but she didn't say a word.

Pansy turned her attention back to me. "You know, Cai, I'd be more than happy to help you with the paper if you'd like."

I shook my head. "It's actually dealing with genetics, not organic chemistry, so Addison is more qualified to review it. Dr. Edison just wanted a second set of eyes on it, someone who understands the science behind it."

I turned toward my computer, but not before I caught Pansy's expression turning to stone. I really hoped this was just Pansy having a bad day, and not another one of her episodes. In the years since I'd known her, every so often, she'd get in these moods where she'd just snap at everyone. It'd happen for a week or two, and then she'd be back to her normal cheery self.

I NEEDED to have a talk with Pansy. It was bad enough when she acted grumpy with people who came in, but I couldn't have her snapping at the staff. It'd never happened before, but I was now wondering if that was just because she'd been controlling herself around people with more seniority or a higher position. Technically, Addison wasn't under Pansy, but Pansy had been here longer.

I just didn't understand how Pansy could take things out on

someone as hard-working and sweet as Addison. Even when she was telling stories or asking questions, she was always working. She'd gotten Dr. Edison's paper back to him in a matter of hours, and he'd called me the next day to tell me that if Addison was at the center, he wanted her looking over his work instead of me.

Apparently, my grammar skills were sorely lacking. While this wasn't exactly news to me, I hadn't realized that my colleagues didn't know it. I supposed that was a good thing. The methods I'd perfected in high school and the first few years of college worked as well now as they had then. Spelling and grammar check first, then hiring someone to read through things. Freelance sites made it easier at least.

I sighed and closed my eyes, rubbing my temples. I had a headache, and as little as I wanted to admit it, Pansy was a big part of it. I'd give her the rest of the week – today and tomorrow was all that was left at least – and if she was still being problematic, I'd talk to her.

Except I didn't know how to talk to her about this. Or anything really. I didn't know how to talk to people in general. I did better with my viruses and gene sequences.

Less complicated.

The moment I opened my eyes, I caught a flash of that fiery color that had my pulse picking up, but Addison didn't come into the lab. Before I could go find out where she'd gone off to, the door to my lab opened. I felt a moment of annoyance, but that vanished when I saw it wasn't Pansy.

It was Dr. Fenster. My boss.

If he was in my lab, something was up. I pushed all other thoughts from my mind, and as soon as he started to speak, I was glad because I needed to focus.

"There's an outbreak in Texas."

TWELVE
ADDISON

MAYBE IT WAS JUVENILE, BUT WHEN I WOKE UP SATURDAY morning, the first thought that had come into my mind was that I wasn't a virgin anymore. It hadn't been some big emotional revelation or me staring at the ceiling with stars in my eyes, the sorts of things that I supposed I would've felt if I'd been in a relationship, or if, at the very least, I'd known the man I'd had sex with.

No, it was more the acknowledgment of the ache between my legs, the sensitivity of my nipples, and the knowledge of how I'd gotten to feel that way. And that was how I'd ended up with an entire weekend of *I lost my virginity to a stranger at a sex club* running through my head.

I hadn't wanted to talk to Dorly or Codie about it either. I didn't regret what I'd done, but I was afraid that if I tried to talk to either of them, they'd think I was upset with them for suggesting it. Or, worse, they'd feel like they pushed me into it. They didn't yet know me well enough to know that no one could ever force me to do something I didn't want to do.

I supposed I *was* still freaking out a little when I got to work

Monday morning, because as soon as I walked into the lab, I started talking and couldn't quit.

Cai didn't seem to mind, at least, and he didn't mind when I did it again on Tuesday. And Wednesday.

I couldn't stop babbling.

When I walked into the lab on Thursday morning, I'd promised myself that I was going to be quiet and let Cai get his work done. But then, he turned and smiled at me, and all my good intentions flew right out the window.

It seemed that even the smoking hot Dominant who'd been filling my dreams couldn't change the way Cai Hunter could turn my brain into mush, and my mouth into a non-stop embarrassment.

"Do you have any other papers you need me to look over?" I asked. "You said Dr. Edison approved the work I did."

"He did," Cai said, "but no one else has asked me for any input. I appreciate you doing that for me."

"No problem," I said with what I hoped was a normal-looking smile and not something from Pennywise the Dancing Clown. "I used to proof my brothers' papers, even Simon's. He's three years older than me, but because I graduated early, I was only one grade behind him in school. I was better at math and science, obviously, so we actually had a few of those classes together."

"Are you getting homesick yet?" he asked, leaning back against his desk as if he had nothing more important to do today than to talk to me.

I shook my head. "No. I'm actually enjoying being able to hang out with my roommate and her girlfriend, make my own schedule that isn't dependent on whether or not I have to babysit or start dinner. Did you have to babysit a lot?"

He shook his head. "We had a nanny."

More evidence that we'd had very different childhoods.

"I have some math I'd like you to review," he said, surprising me.

"Me?"

"I like to have another person go over my information rather than only relying on a computer. The work we do here is too important to risk human or machine error."

He was right. I was here to work, not to get close to him.

I WAS STILL ADJUSTING to life in the South, but I wasn't even close to regretting my decision to move. I was loving work, even with Pansy Kemyss being a pain in my ass. There was always at least one in every workplace, right? Even if you were doing your dream job. That obnoxious co-worker who kept things from being too good.

I would say that I didn't know what her problem was, but I was pretty sure I did know. It was completely misguided, of course, but it also wasn't anything under my control, so all I could do was wait it out until she realized that there was nothing going on between Cai and me. It could've been some sort of professional jealousy, since even though I was technically an intern, I was able to do more of the work than she could, but I saw the way she changed every time she looked at Cai. She had it bad, and I doubted he even noticed. If she hadn't been so petty with me, I would've felt bad for her.

It was only Thursday afternoon, but I was already looking forward to the weekend. Part of me was even considering talking Codie and Dorly into taking me back to the club, but I knew that would just end badly. I'd either find the same guy, and he wouldn't want to be with me again, or I'd find another guy, and he'd be a disappointment. Better to just be happy with what I had and focus on work.

Still, not having to put up with Pansy for two wonderful days was reason enough to look forward to the weekend. Even if it also meant I didn't get to see Cai.

Speaking of Dr. Hunter...

His expression was serious as he came into the break room. "Are you in the middle of something?"

I shook my head. "Just getting something to drink. Do you want anything?"

Idiot. He was standing right here. If he wanted something, he'd get it himself. He wasn't one of those people who thought they had to be waited on hand and foot because they were so much smarter than everyone else.

"Dr. Fenster just came to see me."

Dr. Fenster? The head of the CDC? Shit. Had I done something *that* wrong that the head of the center was here to fire me? Or was I reading too much into this and it wasn't about me at all?

"There's an outbreak in Pecan Grove, Texas. You have an hour to go home, pack what you'll need for a few days, and then get back here."

I had to have misunderstood him. He couldn't have meant I was going with him. "What?"

"Dr. Fenster told me to pick a couple people to bring with me as part of my team. There's a possible chemical aspect, so Pansy's going, but I want you coming as my number two. We're flying out in ninety minutes, so we can begin the initial investigation. The rest of the team is in Massachusetts and will be flying down later this evening."

Without another word, he turned around and walked out, leaving me staring after him, speechless.

The paralysis lasted nearly a full thirty seconds before my brain kicked in, and I went for my purse. In theory, I'd known this was possible. I was an intern, true, but I was almost a doctor myself, and I'd been assigned to a specific scientist, and if he was called to the field, then I could be expected to go with him.

I just hadn't expected it within my first two weeks.

My mind was racing as I hurried outside, the thoughts chasing each other. I should've had a go-bag already prepared. What should I put in a go-bag? The basics were obvious. Toothbrush, toothpaste, brush, soap, shampoo. I should've kept travel sizes on hand. Dorly might have some, but if she didn't, I could take a risk and hope the hotel would have them. Except, I didn't know if we'd be in a hotel. Texas wasn't a third-world country, but I wasn't deluded about the conditions we might encounter. There was a high probability that I could end up sleeping on chairs or a cot; if I slept at all.

Still. Toothbrush, toothpaste, brush, soap, shampoo. Those would work just as well in a public bathroom as it would in a hotel. I didn't know how many days we'd be gone, but I could wash clothes in a sink if necessary, so one pair to wear, one to change into.

I was still making my mental list when I arrived at the apartment.

"Is something wrong?" Dorly asked, concern on her face. "You're back early."

I shook my head, rushing past her into my bedroom. I shouted over my shoulder, "I've got to pack!"

"Pack?" Codie appeared in the doorway. "Where are you going?"

"Texas." I pulled my suitcase out of my closet and set it on my bed.

"Slow down, Addison." Dorly came inside. "What are you doing?"

I stopped, took a deep breath, then let it out slowly. She was right. I needed to slow down. If I kept going at this rate, I'd end up packing six pairs of shoes and my deodorant but forgetting everything else.

Deodorant.

That had to be on my go-bag list for the future.

I needed to make a list.

Not now though. Now, I needed to pack because I didn't have much time before I needed to get back.

"There's a possible epidemic in Texas," I said. "The CDC is sending out a team, and I'm going."

Dorly's eyebrows shot toward her hairline. "They're sending an intern with two weeks of experience into the field to handle an epidemic?"

I rolled my eyes. "It's not like they're sending me out to the deepest darkest jungle with a first-aid kit and a flashlight. There's three of us going out in about an hour. I'll only be helping with initial investigation before the remainder of the team gets there."

"Would your hot doctor be one of the ones going?" Codie asked with a smile.

I glared at her as I stuffed a couple pairs of panties and bras into my bag. "I don't have a hot doctor, Codie. But if you're asking if Dr. Hunter is going to Texas, yes, he is. That's why I'm going." I pointed at her before she could speak. "Because he's my supervisor. That's *all*."

And that was what I reminded myself as I finished packing a few more necessities. This was a business trip. Nothing else.

THIRTEEN

CAI

I was impressed with how quickly Addison returned, and how frugally she'd packed. Most of us, on our first time out, tended to over-pack, preparing for any contingency.

"Dammit!" A harsh curse came from the front door, and I looked over to see Pansy struggling with a massive suitcase as well as a shoulder bag that was almost the same size as mine.

"Did I under-pack?" Addison asked from behind me. "I wasn't sure if there was anything outside the basics I should bring. I can go get my laptop from the lab. Files, books, anything else you think we might need."

I held up a hand before she could start babbling again. "A laptop is a good idea, since you'll want to be able to take notes about anything we find. But we usually encourage whoever is first on site to pack light since they never know what they're getting into. If you've forgotten something, we let the incoming doctors know, and they'll bring it."

She nodded, eyes wide. She didn't look nervous though. At least, that didn't appear to be the primary emotion she was feeling. She looked...*excited*.

"Will this be your first time in Texas?"

Why couldn't I stop talking to her?

"I've never been anywhere except Minnesota and here," she said. "And not much more than around Minneapolis."

"Minneapolis? Who in the world would want to go to Minneapolis?" Pansy said breathlessly as she plopped her bags down next to Addison.

I intervened before Addison could respond, or Pansy could say something worse. "The pilot called a few minutes ago to say that they were almost done refueling. The car to the airfield will be here soon."

"Where, exactly, are we going in Texas?" Pansy asked. "Austin? Dallas?"

"Pecan Grove," Addison answered.

At least one of them had been listening.

"How long are we going to be there?" Pansy put her hand on my arm, and I turned to look at her. "I'm just asking because I remember when we were in Seattle two years ago, we thought we were only going for three days, but we had to stay for five days, and my pet-sitter charged me overtime."

"You know that we won't know anything until we actually get on site." I tried to keep the annoyance out of my voice, but it wasn't easy. Pansy had been here for as long as I had. She'd been at half a dozen sites herself, and we never knew anything for certain until we could assess the scene ourselves.

I remembered the case that she was talking about, as well as her behavior when she realized we'd be staying longer than she'd anticipated. She'd been furious, ranting at anyone who would listen that she couldn't stay in Seattle because she had to get home. She had plans and responsibilities. And I was the one she'd come to about all of it, even though I hadn't been running point on it.

I'd been ready to send her back just to get her away from me.

I really hoped this wouldn't be a repeat.

THREE PEOPLE WERE WAITING outside the Texas hospital when we got there. A short, harried-looking woman in a business suit, an African-American man in scrubs, and a pretty, tired-looking woman. Their expressions when we came toward them told me that they were the ones who'd been dealing with the patients so far. Their faces lit up with the sort of hope that always made me a little anxious. It reminded me too much of the way Slade and Blake had looked at me when we were little, and before our parents died.

Like I could do anything.

That changed after the accident. I didn't know if it was because my brothers no longer believed in me, or because I no longer believed.

"Hi, I'm Dr. Hunter." I held out my hand, and the woman in the suit shook it.

"I'm Isis Bairstow, head of St. Mary's. This is Dr. Neilsen Hoskins. He's been working on this since the beginning." She gestured to the other woman. "And Nurse Diaz was here when the first patients were brought in."

"This is Addison Kilar and Pansy Kemyss, two members of my assessment team." I gestured to both women. "Why don't you get us up to speed and show us where we can set up?"

"Very well," Ms. Bairstow said. "Follow me. We'll talk as we walk."

Efficient. I liked that.

"Dr. Hoskins, do you want to explain?"

"Go ahead," the doctor said. "I'll speak up if I think you've missed anything."

"Three days ago, four men came into the ER with ulcers on

their hands and wrists, as well as irritated, inflamed eyes and swollen lymph nodes. They were admitted for observation. The next morning, three women and two children came in with sore throats, mouth ulcers, tonsillitis, and swollen lymph nodes, as well as a cough. When we discovered that the five new patients were related to the original four, we suspected something transmittable and quarantined them together. Three of the patients began having breathing issues by that night."

"We did blood work, but we're still waiting for results for anything more exotic than the basics," Dr. Hoskins said.

I raised an eyebrow. "After four days?"

"Our lab's had some issues as of late, and it takes forever to get anything back," Nurse Diaz put in.

"Last night is when things started to get bad," Ms. Bairstow said. "A group of six kids were brought in with coughs, difficulty breathing, and chest pain. One of the boys happened to be related to the families in quarantine, which made us believe that all the cases are related. The men with the ulcers have been having issues breathing today."

"I don't think they have much time left," Dr. Hoskins said.

Ms. Bairstow pointed. "We're going to the top floor."

As we crowded into the elevator, Pansy took the silence as an opportunity to start asking the questions that had apparently been forefront in her mind.

"Where are we going to put our luggage? I don't want anything to get lost or stolen. That reminds me, who's going to be taking our things to the hotel? I want to get a name so if anything's missing, I'll know who to talk to. And I need a ground floor room with a handicapped bathroom. I can't handle those little ones."

"Pansy." I didn't yell, but my voice was sharper than usual. "Let's focus on the patients rather than our suitcases."

She gave me the same look she gave whenever I was forced

to reprimand her. On the surface, she appeared hurt, but I could see something...*meaner* underneath. Something I'd begun recognizing a lot more since Addison had joined the CDC.

"This is our floor," Ms. Bairstow said. She stepped out first and waited for the rest of us to join her before starting down the corridor at a brisk pace. When we neared the end, she stopped and pushed open a door to the right. "You can use this as your lab. We don't really have equipment, but there's space in here."

"We have our own," I said. "We'll need all of the charts, x-rays, results of any tests you've run."

"Already ahead of you," Dr. Hoskins said. "They're lined up in the order we saw the patients."

I set down my bag next to one of the chairs and saw Addison do the same. Pansy claimed the couch but didn't say anything. None of us did because before anyone could, Nurse Diaz collapsed.

FOURTEEN

ADDISON

One blink.

Two blinks.

That was all the time I allowed myself to be surprised, and then I was moving. I went to my knees next to the nurse even as everyone behind me reacted.

"Adrionna!"

I took a guess and assumed that was the nurse's name, so I used it when I leaned over her. "Adrionna? Can you hear me?" I put my fingers against the pulse point in her neck. "Her pulse is erratic," I said. "And her breathing's labored."

"Are you a medical doctor?" Dr. Hoskins crouched down next to me.

"No," I moved out of his way to allow him to get to her. "My youngest sister is epileptic, and I spent a lot of time babysitting her. I learned a bit more than usual about first aid."

"Let's get her up," Cai said from behind me.

I stood up, letting Cai and Dr. Hoskins lift the unconscious woman onto the gurney someone had found. The doctor pressed his fingers against Nurse Diaz's neck and frowned. "Her lymph glands are swollen. This is how the kids presented when they first came in." His face looked even wearier than it had just a few minutes ago. "Does this mean we're all going to get sick now?"

"Let's get her into quarantine," Cai said. "Do you have a mask? We'll want to do full precautions from here on out, but we need to get her inside with the others and get her stable."

"Here." Ms. Bairstow passed around high filtration masks, and we all put them on before moving toward the hallway.

"I'll get us set up in here," Pansy said, her voice slightly muffled by the mask. "I won't be any help in there."

Cai didn't even acknowledge her as he pushed the gurney down to the zippered part of the plastic sheeting across one whole section of the floor, and I took my cue from him. Nurse Diaz was the priority. Cai asked Dr. Hoskins questions at such a rapid-fire pace that I could barely follow them, and the expression on the doctor's face suggested that he was having as difficult a time as I was. I made a mental note to suggest to Cai that Dr. Hoskins get some sleep and some food before he passed out from sheer exhaustion.

Ms. Bairstow unzipped the plastic and allowed us to pass through into the anteroom, a small space between the hall and quarantine. We replaced the mask with higher quality respirators, then quickly pulled on protective jumpsuits, face shields, and gloves. Dr. Hoskins opened the second barrier, and we stepped inside. I had a moment to process two rows of beds, and then we were pushing the gurney into an empty space.

"Oxygen." Cai gave the instruction even as Dr. Hoskins was reaching for the oxygen tubing.

The two of them worked together to get the mask on Nurse Diaz, and I busied myself with taking inventory in case they needed anything else. Pulling open drawers and cabinets, I was happy to see that they had a lot of basics, which was good, but if we needed anything a bit more obscure, we'd be in trouble. I started a list in my head of all the possible instruments we might need so I could ask Ms. Bairstow before giving Cai the list.

"Do you have access to Ms. Diaz's health records?" Cai asked as he assisted in inserting an IV and the leads necessary for patient monitoring. "I need to know if any pre-existing conditions may have played a role."

"We don't have enough computers to spare one for quarantine," Dr. Hoskins said. "And we didn't think it'd be wise to carry one back and forth."

Cai nodded and watched the monitor as it began to pick up the nurse's vital signs. "Good call. Until we know more about how this transmits, we'll need to be extremely careful about what we take in and out of here."

"Do we have a hard copy of protocols?" I asked as I held out a stethoscope I'd found and wiped down with alcohol preps.

Cai took it without looking at me. All his attention was focused on the patient. "Ask Pansy. She's responsible for bringing them, making copies, and ensuring that they're properly distributed."

Pansy. Great.

"She's waking up," Dr. Hoskins said. "Adrionna, can you hear me?"

She nodded slowly, her hands moving across the gurney as if she was trying to figure out where she was.

"Do you think you can breathe without the oxygen mask?"

She nodded again, then tried to sit up. Cai put a hand on her shoulder and gently pushed her back down. "Take it easy. Just lay back and answer our questions."

"Do I have it too?" Her voice was surprisingly calm. "Whatever it is these patients have?"

"It's possible," Dr. Hoskins confirmed grimly. "You were having problems breathing, and your lymph glands are swollen."

Cai straightened and looped the stethoscope around his

neck. "Do you have any pre-existing conditions that might have made you more susceptible?"

She thought for a moment. "Asthma, but that's about it."

He nodded. "That would explain the difficulty breathing. How do you feel now?"

"I thought I was coming down with a cold," she said, glancing at Dr. Hoskins. "My throat's been sore all day, and my eyes have been dry."

"We're going to need to keep you in quarantine," Cai said. "Just to be on the safe side. We don't know yet how this bacteria or virus spreads." He turned to Dr. Hoskins. "We're going to want to monitor you and Ms. Bairstow. We need both of you to take care of yourselves, so eat, sleep, stay hydrated, but you need to do all of that from the hospital."

I opened a cabinet and pulled out a hospital gown that looked like it'd fit the nurse.

"What if we were already exposed? Could we have given it to everyone we've seen over the last few days?" Dr. Hoskins asked.

"I don't believe so," Cai said. "But we'll want to put together timelines for you, Nurse Diaz, and Ms. Bairstow so we can compare them with the timelines for each of the other patients. Often, that helps us determine the origin of the infection."

I held up the gown so Adrionna could take off her shirt without embarrassing herself.

"We didn't get much in the way of histories from the kids," Nurse Diaz said quietly.

"Were they unconscious?" I asked as I helped her slide the gown on and tie it.

"They've been in and out," she said. "But I think most of it is because they didn't want to get into trouble. Whatever they'd been doing, it wasn't something they wanted their parents to know."

I thought of my younger sisters, Angel and Erin. At ten and eight, they were hardly rebellious tweens, but like most kids, they did things on occasion that they wanted to hide. But as long as they felt like they would get in more trouble for what they'd done rather than lying, they wouldn't share.

Cai tapped the temporary garments we were wearing. "Our suits are in one of the large cases on the plane."

"You'll want to talk to Ms. Bairstow about that," Dr. Hoskins said.

"All right." Cai put the stethoscope down on a counter. "Nurse Diaz, we need to run some tests on you to compare to the other patients."

She nodded. "Do what you have to do, Doc."

"I'll draw the blood," Dr. Hoskins said. "You two should probably keep your exposure in here to a minimum until you get those hazmat suits, right?"

Cai glanced at me as if he was just realizing that I was still there. "Right. Run all the same tests on her as you did on the others. If there's anything new you want to run, do it, but also do it to the others. We need as many statistics as possible to compare so we can find the pattern."

Cai and I stripped off the protective clothing in the ante-room and used a healthy measure of hand sanitizer, hoping the precautions had been enough.

When we were finished, we made our way back to the hallway where Ms. Bairstow and Pansy were waiting. The head of the hospital was pale as she chewed the side of her lip. Pansy just looked bored and annoyed.

"Ms. Bairstow, I'm guessing you heard my discussion with Dr. Hoskins."

"I did," she said stiffly.

"What I need you to do is remove anything you were wearing when you went into quarantine, take a shower and use the strongest antibiotic soap you have, then change into something clean. Once we have more answers, we'll be able to tell you if you can have your things back. Continue to wear the mask. It's as much for others' safety as it is your own." Cai's voice was clipped, but not cruel. Time was precious in situations like this. "Addison and I will also need to use the showers, then we'll change into our own protective gear from the plane."

"Your cases are in the other room," Ms. Bairstow said. "The ones you were asking about."

Cai nodded, his mouth tight. "Good. At this point, only the five of us will be allowed in that room, and if it's at all possible, I'd like you to refrain from going in there at all. The rest of us will have suits to use from here on out."

"The rest of us?" Pansy spoke up. "I'm not a doctor. Why would I be going in there? And *she's* not a doctor either. I don't even see why she's here."

I didn't need to look at her to know she wasn't referring to Ms. Bairstow.

Cai ignored her. "I'll need access to your entire system. We need to figure out what this is, but we also need to know where it came from, or we risk another outbreak that may spread faster."

"Of course," Ms. Bairstow said. She was still pale but hadn't freaked out, so that was a good sign.

Cai turned to me. "I need you to organize the information regarding the patients' relation to each other, when they were brought in, and what symptoms they displayed at the time of admittance. You also need to find out what new symptoms they might have now, and what they've eaten since the time they first started feeling sick."

I nodded. It sounded like a lot of work, but it was compiling information. I'd always had a knack for statistics.

"Pansy, I need you to come up with a complete timeline.

Start a full five days before the first patient was admitted and work up until today. I want to know who was where at what time. Be as specific as possible. Put it all on the big whiteboard in the other room."

"It's nearly seven o'clock," Pansy said. "Should we get settled in our hotel room first? The information isn't going anywhere."

There was a moment of silence, and then Cai spoke, "Miss Kemyss, you've been brought here to do a job, not to be on a vacation. If you're not comfortable with the work I've given you, you're welcome to return to Atlanta and hand in your two-week notice."

Two spots of color appeared on her cheeks. "That's not what I meant," she mumbled. "I'll do it."

"All right," Cai said. "Let's get to work."

FIFTEEN

CAI

I sighed and pressed the palms of my hands against my eyes until spots danced behind my closed eyelids. I always forgot eye drops. Every time I'd gone on a trip like this, I inevitably ended up with my eyes red and irritated from fatigue and work. And every time, I promised myself I'd remember to add eye drops to my go-bag, and every time, I forgot.

I stretched my arms over my head and listened to my joints pop, my muscles groan. It was Saturday morning, and I'd slept for less than an hour since we arrived Thursday evening. I'd asked for four more team members to come along with a few more specialized pieces of equipment, and they should have been here late yesterday morning. I hadn't, however, factored in the damn nor'easter that had hit New England, grounding my entire back-up team.

It had been a mistake to bring only Pansy and Addison. I should have factored in the storm and planned accordingly, but my mind hadn't been functioning at peak performance.

I stood up, wincing as the chair legs screeched against the tile floor. It was too quiet in here. I always had a hard time working when it was quiet. My thoughts had the tendency to scatter if I didn't have something to distract them.

"Cai, would you like some donuts?" Pansy's voice echoed in the room, and I scowled.

"Shh." I gestured toward the cot at the far corner of the room but didn't look. I'd caught myself staring at Addison at various points over the last few hours, watching her sleep. I definitely didn't need to be doing that right now.

"Shouldn't she be waking up sometime soon?" Pansy lowered her voice, and then she threw one of the dirtiest looks I'd ever seen in Addison's direction. "I mean, this is part of her job, right?"

I hadn't had nearly the amount of sleep I needed to handle her commentary right now. "She's only been sleeping for a couple hours. Leave her."

Pansy rolled her eyes but didn't say anything else. She held out a plate with one hand and a Styrofoam cup with the other. I took the donut on top without paying attention to what it was. The coffee was so bad it made me want to choke, but it was hot and had caffeine, so I kept drinking it.

"Were you able to find that map I wanted?" I asked.

"Apparently, the only place that has the specific map you're looking for is the library, and it doesn't open until ten." Pansy sat down on a chair and smoothed down her skirt. "Which means I'm free to help you here."

Wonderful.

I put down my half-eaten donut and walked over to the big whiteboard that hung on the wall above the cot. I told myself that I was only interested in the information there, not the woman asleep under it, and for once, I listened.

The timeline started with four men who lived on the outskirts of town heading out for a weekend hunting trip. One of the men owned a cabin where the men spent Friday through Monday. According to the paperwork, one of the men noticed the first ulcer on Sunday night. By Monday morning, all four of them had at least two ulcers. They arrived at the hospital six hours later.

Pansy had put the main events on the board, but Addison had written notes in as we'd discovered more information, giving me a fuller picture of the movements of each of the patients for the past week. While the second wave of patients were related to some of the first, the four original patients weren't related to each other. And of the six children, only one was connected to the other patients.

"What am I missing?" I muttered as I paced the length of the room, reading each event from the timeline over, and over again. "Hunting. Home. Sick. Hospital."

I took a step back, as if it would change my perspective enough to show me whatever it was I should've been seeing.

"What did I miss?" Addison sat up, combing her fingers through her hair and blinking the sleep from her eyes.

"Nothing," I answered her question. "You've missed nothing but my absolute failure to do my fucking job." I sighed, running both of my hands through my hair. "Sorry about that. I'm just frustrated."

"You're too hard on yourself," Pansy said, gripping my arm. "After all, you're doing all this work on your own. I wish I could help more."

I shook off her hand and kept talking to Addison. "I'm still waiting for results from the lab. The tests I'm running won't be done for a while, which means there's nothing more I can do there. If I could just figure out the source..."

I scratched at the stubble on my cheeks and refrained from cursing again.

Addison yawned as she stood. "Coffee?"

"There's a vending machine down the hall," Pansy said. "Take your time."

"You can finish mine," I said, holding out the half-empty cup. "It's awful, but it'll help wake you up."

She drained it with one long swallow, made a face, then shook her head. "Yeah, that woke me up." She tossed the cup into the closest trash can and then moved over to stand next to me. "Do you think there's something you're not seeing, or something you're missing from the actual timeline?"

"There's nothing missing," Pansy snapped. "I know how to take notes."

"I'm not saying you did anything wrong," Addison said calmly. "We both took histories, and we could've asked all the right questions, but that didn't mean we got the answers we needed."

"Because the answers might not have been there," I added.

"That," Addison said, "and the fact that people lie. Maybe not everyone or all the time, but they do."

It hit me like a brick. And it'd been right in front of my face this whole time. "Damn kids."

"What?" Addison threw me a funny look.

I walked a foot or so further down the timeline and pointed to a space marking a couple hours before the kids were brought in to the hospital.

"Went for a bike ride."

Addison nodded. "Yes. That's what the kids all said."

"Exactly how did they say it? You said you remember everything. Give me word for word what they said."

"All right." She thought for a moment and then began to recite, *"Wally asked me after school if I wanted to go for a bike ride with him and a couple friends. We met at Wally's house and rode down to the dollar store where we bought some candy. Then we rode out to the river and threw rocks into it for about an hour. Then we went home."*

"Which one of the kids said that?"

Addison frowned, as if she'd just realized something. "All of them. Except for a couple filler words like 'uh' and 'like,' they all said the exact same thing."

"That doesn't happen," I said, pressing my fingers to my temples. "Not naturally."

Her entire body sagged. "I can't believe I didn't see it."

I put my hand on her shoulder before I thought better of it. I waited a couple seconds before dropping it, hoping she'd think it was just me being tired. "You can't blame yourself. You're new to this. Sometimes, taking a history is a lot like conducting an interrogation, or questioning a witness on the stand. You'd think people would always tell the truth when their life was on the line, but that's not the case."

"I'll go talk to Wally again. My gut says he's the leader of the group." Addison turned to go.

I reached out and caught her hand, giving myself a little jolt before I released her. I'd meant to grab her arm, I told myself. Grabbing her hand had been an accident.

"I'll go."

"Let me." Addison didn't look at me as she flexed her hand. "I think I can convince him that he's not going to be in any trouble."

"What makes you think that's why he lied?" Pansy asked, crossing her arms under her breasts. "Some kids just like to lie."

"Maybe," Addison said, "but most kids lie when they're scared. Usually when they think they'll be punished."

"I agree," I said. "Go talk to him."

After she left, Pansy came back over to my side. "Do you really think it's a good idea to let an intern do that?"

I ignored her, tired of her constant second-guessing everything to do with Addison. When we got back to Atlanta, I'd deal with it. For right now, I had people to save.

I STARED AT ADDISON. "They did *what*?"

"They broke into what they thought was Wally's dad's hunting cabin, but what turned out to be the attached shed where Wally's dad and his friends cleaned the animals they'd killed." She wrinkled her nose. "When Wally realized where he was, he and two of the older kids decided to scare the younger ones with some of the bits and pieces the men had left behind."

"That's disgusting," Pansy said.

That, I agreed with.

"Does this mean it's a disease spread through the animals? Their blood and viscera?" Addison asked.

I lifted a shoulder, thinking through all the possibilities. "I'm not sure."

"No," she said, "it can't be only through contact with the animals or their carcasses. It wouldn't explain Nurse Diaz. How would she have come into contact with any of that?"

Dammit.

"You're right. It doesn't give us the exact source. But it does give us a starting point." I looked over at Pansy. "I need you to go to the cabin and take samples."

She made a face. "Wait until the other agents get here."

"We can't. We've got two men on ventilators, and a couple others who'll probably be on them before the night's out. I'll go."

"You can't." Addison popped to her feet. "I don't have

nearly enough experience to work on a cure myself, but I can take samples."

I cursed the damn storm, willing it to abate so the rest of the team could get here.

The thought of her being out there alone, in a place that could be teeming with whatever infection had more than a dozen people in quarantine...it bothered me on a level I didn't like.

"Pansy will go with you," I said and gave the woman a hard look, daring her to complain again. "Even though she currently doesn't act like it, she's been in the field enough that she can help you. Both of you, suit up."

SIXTEEN

ADDISON

I didn't like this. In fact, I hated it.

I was in a full hazmat suit with a hood and gloves and an air filtration system, standing in the middle of a shed that reeked of blood and shit...and that had nothing to do with why I hated my life at this moment.

No, that honor went entirely to the woman sulking next to me.

"Don't get any ideas." Pansy broke the silence after nearly fifteen minutes of following me as I took samples.

"I think Cai appreciates any input he receives about the case," I said, pretending to misunderstand what she meant. I hoped she'd take the out, because this wasn't a discussion I wanted to have.

"You know very well that's not what I'm talking about."

It appeared we were going to go there. I sighed. "Pansy, we're doing something really important here. Can this wait until we're back home?"

"No, it most certainly can't."

I was going to kill Cai for insisting Pansy come with me.

"And it's Dr. Hunter, not Cai," she said stiffly. "You

shouldn't attempt to make yourself more familiar with him than is appropriate."

"You call him Cai," I pointed out as I leaned down to take a swab of a streak of blood. I slipped the swab into a collection tube before dropping it into a plastic bag and straightened.

"Because he and I have been friends for years," she said. "Besides, my relationship with Cai isn't any of your business."

I turned so I could look at her. "You're right, it isn't. The same as my relationship with him isn't any of yours. If he has a problem with me, he can tell me himself."

"You don't have a relationship with him," she hissed, stepping closer, her gloved hands clenching. "And you never will. He's just too polite to say it."

I glared at her for a moment before turning away. I spotted a piece of bloodied fur and used my tweezers to pick it up and deposit it in another bag. "I'm here to work, Miss Kemyss. My interest in Dr. Hunter is purely professional. He's a brilliant doctor who works in a field similar to mine. I've admired his work for years."

Unfortunately, even that didn't shut her up.

"I see the way you look at him, you know. You think he's attractive."

I threw a look over my shoulder before swabbing some mud. "I'm not blind. Of course, I think he's attractive. That doesn't mean I'm going after him or want anything other than an opportunity to see how his mind works."

Pansy snorted a laugh. "I'm sure that's what you want."

I blew out a frustrated breath. "You don't know me. Please don't pretend you do. I'm here to do a job, not to get between you and him."

"Like you could," she muttered under her breath.

This place was filthy. Dirt and layers of dried blood on the floor. The table had newer blood caked on top of old. Bits of guts and fur stuck to the top. A knife was stuck in one corner, the blade dulled with blood.

"You need to request a transfer," she said.

Enough.

I turned around to face her. "No, Miss Kemyss. I am *not* requesting a transfer. I will continue to work for Dr. Hunter until my internship is done or he wants me to transfer to another doctor. Whatever issues you have with him, you need to work out on your own, because they aren't my concern. The *only* thing I'm concerned about is getting the samples that Cai needs to figure out what's wrong with those people, and how to fix them. I'll continue to do whatever he asks of me because he's my supervisor." I let silence hang for a moment before asking, "Are we done?"

"Yes," she said mulishly.

"Good."

I turned back around, completing my pass by stopping next to a pile of...well, of a lot of stuff I either couldn't, or didn't want to, recognize. I took a sample, then stepped over it to reach the door.

I jerked to a stop, stumbling back a step. My brain spun, trying to figure out what had snagged my suit. My foot came down on a piece of what looked like rabbit hide, and I slipped. My hands flew out, trying to find anything to stop myself from falling. I managed to grab onto the doorknob, preventing myself from going to my knees. The bag hanging over my arm swung back and forth, hitting my hip. Thankfully, I didn't have any liquid samples inside.

I took a breath and tried to get my feet under me. It wasn't until I was halfway around to warn Pansy to be careful that I realized the air tasted different. Rancid. Rotten. Putrid. All the words that brought with them the foul, heavy stench now filling my suit.

Horror filled me as I realized what it meant.

"Oops."

I looked up to see Pansy standing in the middle of the pile I'd almost fallen onto. She had an unpleasant smile on her face... and my air hose in her hand.

She'd just exposed me to whatever shit was floating around this shed. On purpose. With a smile.

"You really should be more careful, Miss Kilar."

SEVENTEEN

CAI

THE REST OF THE TEAM HAD GOTTEN HERE ABOUT THIRTY minutes ago, and I'd finished briefing them less than five minutes ago. At this point in a regular case, I would've excused myself for some food and sleep, letting the others pick up where I left off. I'd get several solid hours of sleep, refreshing my mind, and then be ready to join back in as soon as I woke up.

But this wasn't a regular case, not anymore.

I'd found an empty room away from the rest of the team, and now I paced there, trying to work up the nerve to go to quarantine.

No one blamed me – or at least they said they didn't – and I knew that, logically, I couldn't have known what would happen when I'd sent Addison and Pansy into the field together.

It didn't stop me from running through a thousand ways things could have gone differently. I could have insisted Pansy go alone to take the samples. Or have let Addison go alone even though it would have distracted me, knowing she was alone in a strange place, doing a job she'd never done before. It was well within the perimeter of her job description. I could have waited for the others and damned the consequences. The delay might not have been deadly, and I wouldn't have spent the last hour and a half pretending to get work done when all I could think about was how calmly Addison had walked down the hall and into quarantine without a word to me.

She wasn't paying attention, Pansy had said. *Rushing around like it was a race or something. She said she wanted to get back to you. The next thing I see, her air hose is loose. I grabbed it, hoping I could get it back to her before any damage was done. I don't know why I thought that since I know what protocol says, but I was only thinking about her.*

She'd said it all with a straight face, and if I hadn't known her for years, I might've been fooled into believing her story. I knew her tells though. A shift of her eyes to the left. Scuffing the toe of her left shoe against the floor. Twisting her fingers together. All those things had told me that Pansy was lying. For a moment, I'd hoped that the reasoning behind the lies had been to protect Addison. Maybe she'd broken protocol and Pansy had been covering for her.

Even as I thought it, I knew that wasn't the case. Pansy had made her dislike of Addison known from the moment the two women first met. Besides, I'd gotten to know Addison well enough that I knew trying to hide a mistake was against her character.

I'd made Pansy stay behind and had gone to quarantine to find out what really happened.

Addison hadn't pointed fingers. *I was almost done and stepped over a pile of waste. I jerked to a stop and nearly fell. When I regained my footing, I realized that I could smell the room. I turned around, and Pansy had my air hose in her hand.*

She'd fallen silent for a minute, her expression telling me that she had some sort of inner debate going on. Finally, she added the rest of the truth.

I didn't see her grab the hose and pull it out. It could have caught on something. But I don't think that's what happened. She said oops *and that I should be more careful. And she'd been smiling when she said it.*

I hadn't wanted to believe it. I still didn't want to believe it. I'd always known Pansy could be mean at times, but that had been beyond pettiness and cruel remarks. Her actions could cost Addison her life.

The very thought made my blood turn to ice.

I tried telling myself that I'd be equally as concerned if it was any other team member exposed to an infection we hadn't yet identified. If I was a little more worried, it was only because Addison was an intern, not one of the doctors who'd signed on for this sort of thing. Plus, I was responsible for having put her in a position to be infected. I hadn't done anything reckless, but it had still been my call.

I'd always been better at avoidance than lying, and now that lack of expertise was coming back to haunt me. Even though I'd always kept my personal feelings out of my professional life – or thought I had – Addison had somehow snuck past my defenses. I'd come to look forward to seeing her each morning. Talking to her as we worked. Her smile and her laugh had become bright spots in my day.

I needed to see her again.

I didn't say anything to anyone when I retrieved my suit, but I saw the puzzled looks. I excelled at my job but interacting with people had never been a strength.

I was unzipping the second barrier when Addison saw me. She'd taken off her suit, leaving her barefoot and in a pair of jeans and a rumpled t-shirt that made her look years younger than her actual age. She came over to meet me as I stepped inside, her expression strained.

"Any news?" she asked as she looked up at me.

"No progress on identification or treatment," I said, wincing at how blunt my words were. "But we have four more people working on it now. We'll have something in no time."

She smiled, but it didn't reach her eyes.

"You should be resting," I said.

"So, should you," she countered, folding her arms across her chest. "Last time I checked, I'd gotten more sleep since we arrived here than you did."

She had a point, but I wasn't going to let her know that. "I'll make you a deal. I'll sit in the chair if you lay on the bed."

"Sit on the bed," she countered.

I sighed, certain that was the best I was going to get out of her. "All right."

We moved back over to the bed she'd claimed as hers, and I sat in the chair as she sat on the bed, facing me. For several long seconds, neither of us said anything, and I wondered if I'd ruined everything between us by putting her in such a risky position.

"It's not your fault," she said, breaking the silence.

"What's not?"

She gave me a skeptical look. "You're far too smart to be playing dumb. You think I don't know why you're here? You're blaming yourself for what happened. It's not your fault. You sent me into the field the same as you would have any other person with the right expertise. What happened out there... you're not to blame."

I noticed she didn't say anything about the specific event. Had she been lying and was now hoping I wouldn't press the issue? That didn't make any sense. The only logical reason I could come up with was that she didn't think I believed her.

"I fired Pansy."

Her eyes widened. "You did what now?"

"Technically, it must come from her direct supervisor, but she intentionally put a team member in danger so there's no question about it," I said. "Justifiable termination. I told her to return to Atlanta and clear out her desk."

She looked stunned. "She admitted that she pulled out my air hose on purpose?"

"Not exactly," I admitted. "And I can't believe that she was trying to hurt you, but she did knowingly let you venture into a dangerous position."

"You're saying that you fired someone you've known since college because you believe she let me go somewhere that was dangerous." Addison shook her head. "You can't expect me to believe that a brilliant scientist like you actually believes that."

I frowned. "I don't understand."

"Yes, you do." She reached over and sipped some water. "What did Pansy say when you asked her what happened?"

I reached up to rub the back of my neck, then remembered that I was wearing a hazmat suit. "She said that it was all you. That you were rushing around, trying to get things done quickly."

A flush crept up her neck and something sparked in her eyes. "That's not true."

"You said yourself that you didn't actually see her do anything," I pointed out.

"I didn't." Her hands tightened into fists. "But the fact that her story doesn't match mine at all tells me that my hunch was right. It wasn't an accident."

"You think that because her series of events isn't the same as yours that she's lying?" I hoped she saw that I wasn't trying to argue with her. I wanted to understand her way of thinking.

"I think that if it'd actually been an accident, she would have told you something that would've made sense with what I said happened. Her telling you that I was rushing, not doing my job properly, she told you that to make you think you'd made a mistake bringing me."

I shook my head. "Why would she do that? It doesn't make any sense."

She laughed, then coughed, reaching for her water again. After she drank some of it, she spoke, "You're joking, right? You really don't see it?"

"See what?" I asked.

She sighed, pushing herself back to lean against the pillows. "I think that's something you should talk to her about. It's not my place."

I puzzled through her statement for a moment. "Perhaps, or maybe it's more important that you know she won't be causing you any more problems at work."

"I still can't believe you fired her."

"I won't have someone on my team I can't trust," I said. "And I don't trust her."

Part of me wanted to say more, to tell her that, as much as I didn't want to believe that Pansy could do something so awful, I believed Addison's version of the story. The reason I fired Pansy had been because I hadn't been sure I could speak with her without shouting. If something happened to Addison because of Pansy Kemyss, I'd never forgive myself.

But I wasn't ready for any of that conversation with myself, let alone her.

"Ms. Bairstow asked how you were doing," I said the first thing that popped into my head. "I thought that was nice of her."

"It is," Addison agreed. "She's been very...*nice* to me. In fact, she mentioned that the two of us should go out to celebrate when this is all over."

I opened my mouth to say something about that being a nice offer, but before I did, I realized exactly what Addison was saying. "She asked you out?"

"Not exactly," Addison said. "But my gaydar's gotten better since I've been spending time with Dorly."

"Who's Dorly?" The name sounded familiar, and I wondered if it was one of the new members of the maintenance staff.

"Oh, my roommate." Addison smiled, her entire face lighting up. "I was a little worried when I moved here because she and I had only talked a bit via text, but we clicked right away. Then I met her girlfriend, Codie, and it just got better because the three of us get along so well."

Dorly and Codie. Not exactly the most common names, especially not when joined together as a pair. And that's how I knew who they were.

"Dorly's a bouncer, isn't she? And Codie's a waitress?"

Addison looked startled. "They are. How do you know that?"

Shit. I painted myself into that corner. Hopefully, Addison didn't know *exactly* what sort of club her friends worked at.

"I met them at work. Their work, I mean."

She didn't laugh or smile. She didn't do anything, actually. She just stared at me, the color draining from her face.

"Watson." Her voice was so soft that I almost missed it. Then I thought I must've misheard her. "I thought you were a Sherlock Holmes fan."

If I hadn't already been sitting, I would've fallen right on my ass.

This couldn't be happening. It had to be some mistake or a weird joke. But it wasn't funny. And there was no way she could know that word, unless...

"It's for James D. Watson, isn't it? The scientist," she said, lifting her hand to cover her mouth. "It was you. That night at the club."

EIGHTEEN

ADDISON

It was him.

It was the man from the club.

He was the man from the club.

Cai Hunter.

I had sex with Cai Hunter.

My boss.

Fuck.

"James D. Watson," he repeated. "Yes. Scientist."

Even through the plastic mask of the hazmat suit, I could see the stunned expression on his face. I was pretty sure I had a similar look on my face because I'd just been completely gobsmacked.

"You didn't know." He made it a statement rather than a question.

"I didn't," I said honestly. "Not until just now, and a part of me can barely believe it. How did I not know it was you? I mean, not many men are that tall. And your eyes. I can't believe that I didn't recognize them. You talked different too. Because if you talked the same, I would've–"

I started coughing, my eyes watering as I reached for my

water. My brain was still rambling as I gulped down a few mouthfuls of the cool liquid, letting it soothe the scratch in my throat.

"Addison?" Cai was on his feet and at my side before I'd regained enough breath to tell him that I was okay.

I wasn't okay though, and I knew it. I'd spent the last few days studying all the symptoms, and I knew I had several of them already. Irritated eyes, swollen glands, an elephant sitting on my chest. I could hide those, but the coughing, I couldn't. I just had to either convince Cai that it was dry in here or distract him. Considering what we'd just discovered, I was going to go with distraction.

I waved him away as I took as deep a breath as I dared.

"I didn't know either," he said quietly. "Not that night, not until you said...what you said."

"I figured," I said, my voice hoarse. "You have too much integrity to sleep with someone you work with."

He looked surprised at the comment, then pleased. "This is why I don't do relationships."

"What is why?" I asked as my breathing returned to normal. Relatively normal, anyway.

He looked away as he perched on the edge of the bed. "Two years after I first came to the CDC, I was on a team sent to this little village in South America. They had an outbreak of what they thought was a strain of typhoid, but some things didn't add up. I was assigned to follow Dr. Lawrence Tighe, this brilliant guy only a few years older than me."

I leaned forward, my own discomfort forgotten.

"On our third day there, Dr. Tighe was pulling out a needle he'd had in a patient's arm when she started having a seizure. The needle went through his suit and into his arm."

Damn.

"It ended up being an exotic strain of a flesh-eating bacteria.

After two weeks, we found a way to cure it, but it was too late for Dr. Tighe."

"Cai, I'm so sorry." I put my hand on his arm.

He nodded. "When we finally returned to Atlanta, his family had already had the funeral, but I went to their house to offer my condolences. His wife was polite, but she told me something that I've never forgotten. She told me that the work we did at the CDC was important, but that I should never mistake it for being safe. She said she'd loved her husband, but she wished she'd never met him."

I was starting to understand where this story was going.

"I decided then that I would never put anyone through what I'd been through, watching my friend die. And I'd never put a woman through what Mrs. Tighe went through." He glanced at me then. "No relationships for me."

"I get it," I said. "A lot of people wouldn't, but I do. I don't do relationships either. I saw too many screwed up ones."

After a moment, he spoke again. "Can I be honest about something?"

"Of course."

"When I said no relationships, I meant friendships too, especially at work." He reached down and took my hand for a moment, giving it a squeeze. "But I messed that up with you. Even before I found out about what happened...that night...I'm going to fix this, Addison. I can't watch...I *won't* watch you... you're more than just another co-worker."

He stood up, but not before I saw the pain on his face. It broke my heart to see it there, but it also sent warmth through me. He didn't see me as a nuisance, or even simply another co-worker. Whatever this strange thing was I'd been feeling between us, it wasn't only me. We had a connection.

Not a romantic one, of course, but a connection nonetheless.

"Where do we go from here?" I asked. "I mean, about what

happened at the club. Do I transfer to another supervisor? Do we have to talk to someone about it? Fill out a form or something?"

"No." He shook his head, the entire top of the suit making the movement too. "What happened, it never should have happened. Not because I didn't enjoy what we did, but because of who we are to each other. Interns and supervisors...it's not done."

I knew exactly what would happen next, and I said it before he could. "We're going to pretend it never happened."

"We're going to pretend it never happened," he echoed.

Just like I was pretending that every inhale didn't take a massive amount of effort. After all of this, I knew I couldn't do anything that could possibly remind him of the friend he'd lost. I couldn't let him be distracted by me. He needed to focus on his work. It wasn't only my life at stake here.

Still, even my determination couldn't stop the coughing fit that left my ribs aching and my breath coming in ragged gasps.

"I'll fix this," Cai said as he eased me back onto the pillows. "You rest. I'm going to get to work, and I'll make you better."

All I had the strength to do was nod.

NINETEEN

CAI

It had been Addison haunting me all along. She was the reason I'd gone to the club, and I found her there even if I hadn't realized it until just now. She'd been the one I'd gone to for a distraction from my mystery lover. This whole time, it had been her.

I refused to lose her.

I meant it when I said that nothing else could happen between us, but I would still have her in my lab, working with me, talking to me. I wouldn't lose that.

I hadn't been able to save Dr. Tighe, but I wouldn't fail Addison.

I headed back to the temporary lab. I needed to sleep, I knew, but I had work to do first. I'd take a nap after I had some tests running. Until then, I'd work.

YESTERDAY WAS a blur of numbers and algorithms, and this morning hadn't been much better. I took apart and pieced together every possible combination of the symptoms I could think of. I tried finding other explanations for things I'd considered symptoms. Was a sore throat a symptom of whatever this infection was, or just something that happened this time of year? Nurse Diaz had asthma, but none of the histories suggested any breathing issues, so I felt safe assuming that was a definite symptom.

The process of elimination was something we had to do whenever we went into a situation where we didn't know what we were dealing with. If we made the mistake of thinking something was a symptom and it wasn't, it could hinder our diagnosis to the point where people could die.

The one positive thing about Addison having been exposed to whatever virus or bacteria was causing our problem was that she could distinguish between how she'd felt before exposure and how she felt after. She'd been able to give a thorough explanation of every ache and sniffle, but since there seemed to be symptoms that she wasn't experiencing, it didn't help as much as I'd hoped.

"Dammit!" I muttered as I pushed back from the desk. I was missing something, and I couldn't figure out what it was.

"Dr. Hunter, are you okay?"

I rubbed the back of my neck as I turned toward Dr. George. He was a nervous-looking guy even when we weren't at an outbreak. Now, he looked like he was just waiting for the zombie apocalypse to erupt from quarantine.

My heart gave a twist. Zombie apocalypse. Addison had joked about that the first time we'd met. I'd thought it was funny at the time. One of the first things I'd laughed at in a long time.

"Anything new?" I asked as I leaned forward and rubbed my temples.

"Patient four was put on oxygen," he said. "He kept refusing, but his numbers were too low, so the doctor put on a mask."

I turned back around and tapped in a few things on my

spreadsheet. It didn't make a difference, but I entered the information anyway. I needed to be thorough. One little miss could be the difference between life and death. In my line of work, the concept of *no pressure* didn't exist.

"It's not too bad here." Dr. Walters walked into the room the same way she walked into every room. Like she owned it, and we all existed to heed her beck and call.

Normally, it didn't bother me. Every doctor had their own quirks, and most of them included some form of arrogance. I knew I had similar tendencies myself.

But what she'd just said...

"*Not too bad?*" I was on my feet before logic caught up to my emotions, but for once, I didn't allow myself to give in to logic. "We have a dozen people who are waiting for treatment, but we can't give it to them until we figure out what the hell is wrong with them. And one of those patients is one of our own. Now, you tell me exactly how the *fuck* is that *not too bad?!*"

Dr. George and Dr. Walters stared at me like I'd grown a second head, and as each silent moment ticked by, I felt more and more like that was the case.

"I didn't mean anything by it," Dr. Walters finally said. "Just that, compared to some of the other places we've been, the outbreak here hasn't kept spreading, and there've been no deaths."

She was right. Half of the time, at least one patient was dead before we were even called in. Dr. Hoskins and Ms. Bairstow had gotten us involved much quicker than a lot of other places would have.

"I apologize," I said. "I haven't gotten much sleep recently."

"Maybe you should take a nap," Dr. George suggested. "Dr. Edison wanted me to wake him up at ten. That's only thirty minutes."

I shook my head. "I need to figure this out."

"Dr. Hunter, we haven't had any new patients since Miss Kilar," Dr. Walters pointed out, her usual bluster tempered. "No new data. There's nothing else for you to figure out."

"Just because no one new has come in..." The sentence trailed off as what she said clicked. "No one new."

"That's right." Dr. George seemed puzzled. "Did you think of something?"

I ignored him and walked over to the whiteboard where the timeline was written. We'd added in Nurse Diaz's and Addison's information, but I hadn't really looked at it because I'd been here when both had been infected. Now, I was thinking that I'd missed something.

Nurse Diaz had been working on all the patients, so we'd assumed that she'd contracted the illness from them. We still didn't know the incubation period, so she could have gotten it at any point in time, but as I scanned the timeline, a picture started to form in my head.

"We know it can't be strictly airborne because Dr. Hoskins is fine, and he was breathing the same air, but there has to be some sort of airborne component because Addison only breathed in the air. She didn't touch anyone other than Nurse Diaz," I mused out loud.

"How can a virus be airborne and not-airborne at the same time?" Dr. Walters asked.

"We don't know that it's a virus," Dr. George said. "The mild fevers suggest infection."

I closed my eyes and tuned them out. I could feel something right at the edge of my subconscious. What was it Addison had said? That she'd stepped on a pile of stuff, smelled the rot, and that's when she realized something was wrong.

An image flashed into my mind. The spring before my parents died, they'd taken us kids on a hike. Blake had been running, jumping, and at one point, he'd landed on a pile of mushrooms. Spores had exploded out of the mushrooms, making him sneeze and cough.

Addison had stepped on a pile of something and breathed in whatever it was that had made her sick. My gut told me that Nurse Diaz had been gathering belongings from each of the patients before they'd been moved into quarantine. She could have easily caused a similar reaction if clothing had contained the same bacteria as what was in that pile.

All the pieces fell into place as that realization clicked home.

Same infection, spread differently, with different symptoms but some crossing over.

"I have an idea."

"IT MAKES SENSE," Addison said. She coughed, turning her face into the crook of her elbow as if I wouldn't notice how hard the coughs were.

I waited until she was done, then handed her a glass of water. I wanted to smooth back her hair, tell her she was going to be okay, but I needed to maintain my distance.

"I can give it to the first patients," I said. "I'm confident it'll work."

"But you wanted to give me the option to try it first."

"You are part of the team," I said. "And I figured you'd never forgive me if I didn't give you the option to play the guinea pig."

"You figured right," she said with a smile. "Are these going into my IV or pills?"

"IV," I said. "I want to get this cocktail into your system as quickly as possible."

The part about my job that I hated the most was the part right after a possible cure was given, when I had to wait to see if it was going to work or not. With Addison being the first, it was worse.

I knew she wouldn't want me hanging around while we waited, and I couldn't justify it professionally, so after I administered my antibiotic cocktail, I excused myself. I should have tried to rest, but I knew I wouldn't be able to sleep, no matter how tired I was.

That, I supposed, was how I found myself on the roof of the hospital, watching the sun set, and calling my brother.

"Cai? Are you all right?"

"I'm fine," I said automatically. Then I sighed and answered honestly, "No, actually, I'm not. I'm in Texas, looking into an outbreak, and my intern is infected."

"Shit. That's rough."

Jax's reaction surprised me almost as much as my calling him had surprised us both.

"Yeah," I said, momentarily unable to think of anything else to say.

"Is there anything I can do?"

"I'm waiting for results of a possible cure," I said. "I should be sleeping, but I can't."

He was silent for a moment, then spoke, "I'm going to build that club I talked to you guys about."

A sense of relief flooded me. He understood. "Did the bar owner cave?"

Another moment of silence. "Not exactly."

"That sounds like a story." I really hoped it was the sort of story that would keep my attention.

He laughed. "It is."

Had my straight-laced, stick-up-his-ass brother of mine just *laughed*? I hadn't heard him like this since...honestly, I couldn't think of a time in our adult lives that I'd had anything like this easy conversation with him.

"The bar burnt down."

I blinked. "What?"

"Some asshole who wanted the bar tried to burn it down with Syll in it, but I got there in time to carry her out. She's okay."

"Please tell me that your story isn't that you hired someone to set the bar on fire, so you could show up and save Syll."

Another laugh, this one longer and louder. "I'm not *that* much of an asshole, Cai."

"I hoped not," I said honestly.

"Relax," he said. "I'd already decided that I was going to let the bar issue drop. It wasn't worth Syll hating me."

"Then how are you building your club? Did you find a new location?"

"Nope. I got Syll out of the bar in time, but the firefighters couldn't put it out fast enough. It was destroyed."

What the *hell* had he been doing since I left Boston?

"After Syll was released from the hospital, I took her back to my place. And, well, long story short, we figured out who tried to kill her."

"That's good," I said as I sat down. It seemed like Jax was having just as odd a time over the past few weeks as I was.

"It is," he said. "Especially considering she's going to be your sister-in-law sometime soon."

"Excuse me, my what?"

"On Saturday, I took her back to the lot to show her that I'd had it cleared and then I proposed. She accepted, and we're going to build a club as equal partners."

What sort of strange alternate universe was this? Because that was the only rational explanation that existed for what Jax was telling me. Granted, he'd been gone over that woman before I left Boston, but *marriage*?

"Congratulations."

I could almost feel him smile. "I know what you're thinking."

I doubted that.

"It was fast, I know," he continued. "But Syll and I...I've never met anyone like her. She just gets me, and she's not afraid to call me on my shit. Have you ever met someone you just clicked with? Someone who you felt so in sync with that the idea of continuing your existence without her just doesn't seem possible?"

Shit.

I had.

TWENTY
ADDISON

I TRUSTED CAI WITH MY LIFE, QUITE LITERALLY, AS IT turned out. I hadn't even thought twice when he told me that he had a potential cure for the infection. I volunteered to be the test subject, and I hadn't let him see for one second how scared I was.

By Monday night, the blood tests showed that the antibiotic cocktail Cai had given me was doing exactly what he'd hoped, and then it was given to the others. I didn't know any of that, though, because I'd fallen asleep shortly after he'd come to see me, and I didn't wake up until Tuesday morning.

Cai was sitting in the chair next to my bed when I opened my eyes. The first thing I noticed was how much easier it was to breathe. The second thing was that Cai wasn't wearing his hazmat suit.

"Cai, what are you–?"

He held up a hand and smiled, his expression weary. "You're not contagious."

"I'm not?" I looked down at my arm where the intravenous tubing continued to pump in what I assumed was more of the cocktail.

"Have you ever heard of tularemia?"

I glared at him. "You're seriously giving me a pop quiz?"

He chuckled. "It's an infection that is contracted in different ways and has various manifestations."

"Ulcers, swollen lymph nodes, sore throat, difficulty breathing, coughing." I listed off several of the symptoms.

Cai nodded. "When you stepped on that pile of detritus out at the cabin shed, it released the organisms in aerosol form. That's what you breathed in when Pansy pulled out your air hose."

"That's how the kids got it too. They were in the cabin."

"Some of it got on their clothes," he continued the explanation. "When Nurse Diaz packed up their things, she inhaled the same thing you did, maybe a little less."

"And the others?" I asked.

"The men came in direct contact with the contaminated animal or animals."

"And the second wave of patients encountered the animal or animals after the hunters brought them home," I finished.

"Exactly. Once I was able to pinpoint how Nurse Diaz was infected, everything fell into place."

"Does that mean everyone else is okay?" I glanced toward the curtains pulled around the other beds.

"They will be," Cai said. "You were the last one infected, so it worked faster on you than it will on them."

"Does that mean we can go home?"

He gave me a *sorry* look. "Not yet. You still must go through another round of bloodwork, so we can make sure the infection is completely gone. The rest of the team is taking care of the cabin and the shed, then they'll return to Atlanta. I'll be staying here until you're discharged sometime tomorrow."

He was staying here with me?

I didn't want to read too much into it, but something told me that he wouldn't have been staying with any of the other doctors. I wasn't sure that meant anything more than us being friends, but it was something.

I WAS beyond ready to get out of the hospital. I'd never been a fan of being a patient, but this was worse. I had nothing to keep me busy, and I kept feeling like I should be up working even though Cai kept reassuring me that there wasn't anything for me to do.

We'd spent most of yesterday talking. I'd dozed off a time or two, but he'd always been there when I woke up, reading a book or making notes. It was odd, I knew, for someone I barely knew to make me feel as safe as he did, but it shouldn't have surprised me. After all, I'd felt safe with him at the club when I hadn't even known it was him.

"Are you ready to get out of here?" Cai said as he came into the room. "I have your test results, and you're all clear."

"That's great." I tried not to let my relief leak into my voice.

"You're going to have to take some time off."

I stared at him, thrown by the sudden change of topic. "What was that?"

"It's part of your contract," he said. "I'm guessing that means you haven't read it since you remember everything you read."

"Are you purposefully being a pain in my ass?" I immediately clapped my hands over my mouth. "I am so sorry."

He laughed. "It's all right. I wasn't exactly explaining things well."

"No, you weren't."

"Let me try that again." He leaned against the wall. "If we're ever exposed to anything while in the field, we're required to take a few days off, the number to be determined by the supervisor."

"*You're* the supervisor," I pointed out.

"I am," he agreed. "And you're going to take the rest of the week off."

I shook my head. "No."

"Yes," he insisted. "And for today, at least, I'm going to make sure that you rest. I've already had our luggage taken to the hotel."

"The hotel?" I echoed.

"The plane is currently in use, so we can either wait here or drive back to Atlanta. I don't know about you, but I don't much feel like renting a car and driving for twelve hours."

"You have a point."

His expression grew serious. "Let's go back to the hotel, get real showers, sleep in real beds, have real food. Then, tomorrow, we can talk about everything else."

"I do like the idea of a shower."

THE ROOM WAS NICE ENOUGH, but I barely saw any of it. I was just happy to be out of the hospital. No beeping monitors. No sharp smell of disinfectants. No murmur of people talking, or the tossing and turning of other patients. But as much as I liked the idea of not being around other people, I didn't want to be alone right now. I'd think too much.

"I'll leave you to it," Cai said as he set my bag down next to the dresser.

"Cai?" I didn't look at him, knowing I wouldn't have the strength to say what I wanted if I faced him. "Will you stay? Please."

"Go get cleaned up," he said quietly. "I'll be here when you get out."

I could feel him watching me as I walked over to the bathroom, but neither of us said anything. I gathered the items I needed for my shower, then closed myself in the bathroom. Despite all the sleep I had gotten over the last couple days, I was exhausted, and I let my brain float as I went through the motions of getting ready.

I turned the heat up until steam filled the room, and then stepped under the spray. I closed my eyes and let all the filth – real and mental – slough off. Shampooing my hair, washing, shaving, all of it was done on automatic pilot. I knew I'd eventually have to truly deal with what happened to me, how much danger I'd been in, but I wouldn't do that today. And I wouldn't deal with the still-present questions about my feelings toward Cai Hunter either.

Not today.

I felt more human as I toweled off, more than I had since I'd gone to that cabin. My clothes had been cleaned, but I didn't put them on, needing something more comfortable. I pulled on one of the hotel robes, then stepped out into the room.

Cai was sitting in the chair across from the bed, his gaze immediately settling on me. His eyes were darker than usual, tension radiating off him. I'd seen that look before, though I hadn't recognized him at the time.

How had I not known it was this man behind that mask?

Need made my stomach clench painfully, but it wasn't hunger for food that had me walking across the room. Any thought or logic that had made it through my shower disappeared, leaving behind a primal desire I was quickly learning only one thing could satisfy.

He watched me as I stopped directly in front of him, his fingers digging into the arms of the chair as I bent down and pressed my lips to his.

TWENTY-ONE
CAI

I TOLD MYSELF THAT WHEN I BOOKED THE ROOMS HERE, this had been the last thing on my mind, but a part of me knew that wasn't entirely true. From the moment I realized that she was the woman behind the mask, having her again had been on my mind. Honestly, that thought had been lurking ever since that night, even before I'd known who she was.

There were a thousand different reasons why this was beyond a bad idea, but only one reason why I wasn't going to stop unless she asked me to – I needed to have her again.

She dug her fingers into my hair, and I grabbed her hips, pulling her down on my lap. I kept one hand on the small of her back and moved the other up to tangle in her wet hair. I swept my tongue between her lips, exploring her mint-flavored mouth. She moaned, squirming on my lap until my cock pressed painfully against my zipper.

It would be too easy to do this right here and now. I wasn't wearing anything under my jeans, and I doubted she was wearing anything under that hotel robe, leaving a button and zipper the only things preventing me from being inside her.

Skin to skin, inside that burning, molten heat. I'd never been tempted to forgo condoms until this moment. The worst part was, it wasn't logic or concern that kept me from doing just that. I just wanted to take my time.

I pulled on her hair, baring her neck so I could kiss and lick every inch. My free hand roamed now, exploring the firm curve of her backside before moving to her long, amazing legs. My fingers crept under the bottom of the robe, and I waited to see if she'd ask me to stop. She didn't, her hands dropping to my shoulders as she gave over control to me.

"Cai," she breathed my name as my hand moved up her thigh. "You feel so good."

I smiled against her throat, then pulled skin between my teeth, worrying at it until I left a small mark. She could cover it with make-up, but I'd know it was there. She'd know too.

I moved my face lower, kissing across her collarbone, then down to the valley between her breasts. I pushed open the robe, my hand tightening on her upper thigh. Her breasts were perfect, from their size to the peach-colored nipples that hardened under my gaze.

I took one in my mouth, sucking on it even as I flicked my tongue across the tip. I was rewarded with a gasp, and then she said my name again. And again. I'd loved hearing her calling me 'Sir' before, and I wanted to hear it again, but not right now. I rarely bedded women who knew my name, so to hear it as she writhed on my lap was sweeter than I'd have imagined it to be.

"Please, Cai, I want...I want...please..." Her hands fisted in my shirt and she tugged at it. "Off."

I chuckled, letting the vibration move across her skin before releasing her nipple. "Patience. I intend to take my time with you." I met her eyes, needing to know one thing before this went any further. "If that's what you want."

She nodded, crushing her mouth against mine hard enough

to bruise. The muscles in her slender body flexed as she wrapped her arms around me. I slid one arm under her ass and the other across her upper back. My tongue tangled with hers as I stood, taking her with me. She yelped in surprise, and I used the opportunity to take control of the kiss. I nipped at her bottom lip, then drew it into my mouth, sucking on it until I reached the bed.

I sat her down on the edge and disentangled myself. Her hair hung in wet locks, twisted and tangled from my rough treatment. Her lips were slightly swollen, her breathing rapid. One of her breasts was still bare, and I reached out and ran my thumb across the nipple.

"That night in the club," I began, "that was the first time you'd had sex."

"Yes."

"Any kind of sex?"

She raised an eyebrow. "Are you asking how far I'd gone in the past?"

I gave her a half-smile. "I suppose I am."

"Not this far."

Good enough answer.

I pulled off my shirt, then went down on my knees in front of her. I kept my gaze on her face, wanting to see her expression as I became the first man to go down on her. I pulled her legs over my shoulders, tugging her closer. Her eyes widened as understanding dawned on her face. She didn't say anything though, watching me as intently as I was watching her.

Her eyelids fluttered as I ran my tongue across her sensitive skin. I teased her, tracing the outline of her lips before dipping the tip of my tongue between them. She moaned, shifting her hips, but I held her steady.

"I'm in control," I said quietly. "Do you remember what you're supposed to say if you want me to stop?"

She nodded. "Watson."

"Good. Now, let go and let me take care of you."

"I want to come."

I smiled and nipped the soft skin of her inner thigh. "I'm sure you do, but I get to decide when that happens. Understand?"

She scowled. "You're bossy."

"Yes, I am," I admitted.

"I could get myself off quicker."

I tightened my hold on her hips. I sincerely hoped she was kidding, because if I had to stop before I could make her climax from my mouth, I was going to hate myself for going into Dom mode. But I would hate myself just as much if I hadn't let her see who I truly was.

"Is that what you want?" I asked, careful to keep the desperation out of my voice. I would honor whatever decision she made, but I'd be lying if I said I wouldn't be disappointed if things ended here.

She reached down and ran her thumb along my bottom lip. "No," she said. "You're in charge. I'll be good...Sir."

Damn.

I caught her hand and drew her thumb to my mouth. I licked it clean before releasing her. "Lie back and relax. Enjoy yourself, because I certainly intend to."

I lowered my head, resuming long, languid strokes that had her moaning my name. Her leg muscles flexed against my back, her heels thumping against my shoulder blades. I could feel the tension building in her body. I could make her come easily, pressure on her clit, a finger inside her, curling to find her g-spot, but I wanted to stretch this out, take her to the edge again and again, teach her how denial could give her the most explosive orgasm she'd ever had.

I wanted to teach her about all my world had to offer. She

would take to it, I knew she would. She'd be the sort of sub I'd always dreamed of having. Submissive, but with steel in her spine and fire in her eyes. Dominating a woman like that was a challenge that appealed to me on a deeper level than merely sexual.

"Cai," she whimpered. She caught some of my hair between her fingers, twisting and pulling until my eyes watered.

"Yes?" I looked up, making no effort to hide my smug smile.

"I'm so close." She reached down between her legs, but before she could touch herself, I caught her wrist.

"Who's in charge?" I asked. I brought her hand to my mouth and kissed her palm.

"You are."

"And who decides when you get to come?"

"You do."

I stood, and she made a noise of protest. "Don't worry. I intend to return to my task as soon as I've made an...*adjustment*."

"What are you talking about?"

I reached down and pulled the belt of the robe free. The sides of the robe fell apart, revealing the pale skin of her flat stomach and a thin strip of auburn curls.

"Hands."

Her eyes darted to the belt, then up to me. I waited, letting her decide without any persuasion, intentional or otherwise. When she held out her hands, a thrill went through me. No matter how impulsive her kiss had been, or even if we were caught up in the moment, she'd made a choice to give me her power, and I wouldn't take that lightly.

I tied her wrists quickly, leaving enough give to prevent her skin from chaffing, but tight enough to restrict her movement.

"Scoot back," I said. I followed with the belt, indicating when she could stop. I pulled her arms up until they were over

135

her head, and then wrapped the free end of the belt through the notch at the top of the headboard. I tied the knot tight, then stepped back to admire my work.

Her body was stretched out, all long lines and lightly freckled flesh. The robe framed her nicely, somehow more alluring than if she'd been completely naked. I planned to have her that way at some point, but right now, this was perfect.

I stripped off my pants and kicked them aside, pausing only to get out my wallet and retrieve my emergency condom. I tossed that on the bed and made a half-joking mental note to check the hotel gift shop for condoms.

"Now, let's see how close I can get you to the edge again."

She glared at me as I climbed onto the bed, but she didn't try to keep me from settling down between her legs. I didn't start slow this time, instead focusing immediately on her clit. Back and forth, circles, the alphabet. Every possible way to torture the sensitive bundle of nerves.

And that was how I learned that Addison didn't only babble when she was nervous. She did it when she was kept from coming, and it was as equally entertaining.

"Please, Cai, I need to come. I'm going to explode. Everything's on fire. Please, please. Sir. Let me come. I'll do anything if you'll just let me come. Anything. I promise. Just tell me what to do, and I'll do it. Please, Cai."

"Anything?" I echoed. "What do you mean by anything?"

"I don't know." Her eyes were as wild and desperate as her voice. "Whatever you want me to do. I'll suck your cock. I've never done it before, but I'm a quick learner. You're too big for me to take all of it, but I'll try. I'll make it good for you, I promise."

Fuck. The thought of sliding my cock between her lips, seeing how deep she could take me, and then pushing it just a bit more...

I could almost come from that thought alone.

"Cai..." My name came out in a whine.

"Just a little longer," I said as I went back to work.

My tongue traced around her entrance, then slipped inside. I'd let her come this time, I decided. Considering this was only her second sexual experience, she was accepting everything I'd asked her to do surprisingly well. I'd tied her up, and she hadn't even blinked.

"Cai, not again. I can't do it again."

I could hear it in her voice, feel it in her body as I took her clit between my lips. She was reaching the point where she couldn't take anything more. If I didn't let her come this time, she'd use her safe word, and she'd never trust me like this again.

"It's all right," I said. "I'm going to let you come this time."

"Thank you," she practically sobbed. "Thank you. Thank you."

She continued to repeat those two words over and over until they turned into a scream. Her thighs clamped down on either side of my head, her entire body arching off the bed, and I softened my touch, helping ease her back down. When she slumped back onto the bed, legs sprawled wide, I moved up to my knees.

"Thank you," she said, her voice hoarse.

I slid my hands up her calves and back down again. She shivered, her skin still sensitive. "Thank *you*."

She was still gasping, so the words came out in pants. "For what?"

My hands moved over her knees to her thighs. "For trusting me to take you there."

She gave me a smile. "I've trusted you to save my life. After that, this was easy."

I nodded, not wanting to think about what would've happened if I hadn't made the connection in time.

"Are you going to let me keep my promise?" She licked her lips.

"Later." I leaned over her and brushed my lips across hers. "Trust me, I'm looking forward to teaching you all the wonderful things you can do with your mouth, but right now, unless you've changed your mind, I need to fuck you."

She blinked, startled by my word choice.

"I don't want to be soft and gentle, Addison," I warned her. "I want to continue to show you how good this can be, but only if you—"

"Yes." She tugged on her restraints. "Yes! No more waiting. Please, Cai. I can't wait anymore. I'm not a patient person. I thought I was, but I'm not."

I opened the condom wrapper and rolled it on as she talked. The next time we did this, I would order her to talk dirty. I had a feeling she'd be quite good at it.

"Are you going to untie me?" she asked as I moved closer.

I cupped her ass, lifting her up until we were lined up, and then I buried myself inside her with one quick thrust. She cried out, but I recognized it as pleasure, not pain. Still, I waited a moment before starting a fast, deep pace that drove me to the very end of her, her body accepting me as if I'd been made to be with her like this.

We were both too close for this to last long, no matter how much I might have wanted it to. I dropped her hips and leaned over her, her nipples hard pebbles against my chest. I rolled my hips, the base of my cock rubbing against her clit. I kept enough of my weight on my arms to keep from crushing her but stayed low enough that I could take her mouth as I drove us toward mutual release.

Then she was there, her body thrashing underneath me, mouth pulling away from mine, so she could yell my name again. She wrapped her legs around me, holding me inside her, tightening her quivering muscles until I came too.

I rolled to the side, tugging her hands free as I went so she could lay next to me, catching her breath too. She snuggled up against my side, and I wrapped my arm around her. We'd have to think about this later, I knew, but for right now, I was going to lay here and enjoy the moment for as long as it lasted.

TWENTY-TWO
ADDISON

THINGS COULD'VE BEEN AWKWARD AFTER CAI AND I HAD sex again, this time knowing who the other person was. But it, strangely, wasn't. I woke up and he was in the shower, but when he came out, he smiled and said he'd call room service for breakfast while I showered.

And food was indeed waiting. A lot of it.

Now, I was in clean, if wrinkled, clothing, eating my third helping of waffles, while Cai sat across the table, working on his own breakfast. Neither one of us had said much of anything yet, but the silence wasn't uncomfortable. More like we understood each other on a level that didn't exist with anyone else.

I wasn't entirely sure how I was supposed to feel about that.

"Why May?"

I looked up, confused by the question. "What?"

"At the club that night, you said to call you May. Why that name?"

I shrugged, feeling a blush creeping up my cheeks. "It's my middle name."

He laughed. "And here I'd been trying to figure out if it was your favorite month or if you were a *Spiderman* fan."

It was my turn to laugh. "Aunt May. I never would've pegged you as a comic book nerd."

He shrugged. "They were an easy escape for me."

I wanted to pursue that train of thought, but I had a feeling it might be a little too serious for the moment. I didn't want him thinking that I felt like I had some right to know personal details about him because we'd slept together.

I went with a question that I'd been thinking about for a while, and that I felt was a little more pertinent to our new level of intimacy.

"How did you get into BDSM?"

He was quiet for a moment, but I didn't get the impression that he was angry, just thinking.

"I've always been a bit of a...control freak. I never did the relationship thing, but even in casual hook-ups, I wanted to be in charge. When I first moved to Atlanta, a woman I'd met took me to the club where you and I first had sex. I felt like I'd found a place where things finally made sense in an area of my life that hadn't before. I understood the rules, the way things worked. It offered order whenever I needed it."

I nodded as he spoke, his words explaining the way I'd been feeling since that night at the club. I wasn't a submissive person by nature, but I found the idea of exerting control over someone else exhausting. I'd spent most of my life having to be the parent, the adult. Even if I hadn't been taking care of other people, I had to take care of myself. With Cai, I'd let him take care of me, let him take charge.

And it had been...freeing.

"I do wonder though," he said, "how much of what we are is formed by our experiences when we are young."

I leaned closer. "What do you mean?"

"Do you ever look at your siblings and see all the ways you're different and all the ways you're the same?"

"Sometimes. Mostly how we're different."

He smiled. "Me too. I've always thought that the four of us boys couldn't have been any more different. Growing up, that's what everyone said all the time. How none of us were alike. We had nothing in common."

I understood that.

"Until recently."

"Your grandfather," I murmured.

He nodded. "That too. But we'd always known that loving him was the only thing we had in common since the accident. When I went back to Boston, I already had in my head that this would be it. That I'd likely never see my brothers again until another funeral. Maybe a wedding."

"What changed?" I asked.

"Before I flew home, the four of us had a conversation that revealed there was one other thing we had in common. BDSM."

I made a face. "Wasn't it weird, talking to your brothers about stuff like that?"

He shrugged. "It's not like we talked about our favorite positions or anything like that. Just the...idea of it."

"I think I'd rather go back to that shed without a suit than talk to my siblings about sex," I said. "Just the thought of it..." I shuddered.

Cai stood and carried his plate back over to the food service cart. "I'm still waiting for a call about the company plane. Do you want to go do something today? It's beautiful outside."

"Outside might be nice," I said. "Is there something you'd like to see?"

He shook his head. "I don't know. I've never been to this part of Texas before. My brother lives in El Paso, but I've never been there either."

From the way his shoulders suddenly tightened, I knew he hadn't meant to say that last bit.

"Did you tell him you were nearby?" I already knew the answer but asked it anyway.

"I love my brothers, Addison, but one fifteen-minute talk about our mutual interest in particular sexual preferences didn't make us close. We went our own ways a long time ago."

I stood and crossed over to where he was, his back still to me. "I know it's not my place, but they're your family. You don't have to let your grandfather's death break you apart more than you are. You can let it be a second chance."

He made a derisive sound. "You sound like my grandfather. He wanted us to make amends. Made it part of his will, in fact. If we want our inheritance, we must reconcile. And his lawyer is going to be the judge of whether or not we've done that."

I told myself that it wasn't my place to put a judgement on his family, but I couldn't help but wonder how tough things must have been if his grandfather had felt the need to take such drastic measures. "Your brother that lives nearby, how do you get along with him? Compared to your other brothers, I mean."

"Slade's pretty easy to get along with," he said. "He just never takes anything but work seriously."

I took a chance and put my hand on his arm. "I think we've had enough seriousness since we've been here. Something, a little lighter sounds like it might be worth a shot."

He didn't answer, but I knew he was thinking about it. He might not have been aware of it, but I'd heard it in his voice. He didn't want things with his brothers to stay the way they were. He wanted to make things right, and I was going to help him do just that.

TWENTY-THREE

CAI

How had I let her talk me into this? I was supposed to be the one in control, but somehow, Addison had convinced me that calling Slade was the best thing to do. I hadn't really expected him to pick up the phone, but he had, and I found myself saying that I'd like to see him while I was in the area. To my surprise, he'd accepted, and that was how I now found myself walking into Tabla with Addison at my side.

She'd argued about coming, but then I'd pointed out that she was the only reason this dinner was happening. It'd taken me threatening to cancel if she didn't come with me, but I'd finally gotten her to agree, under one condition. She wanted to buy something nice to wear.

Nice didn't begin to cover it.

The dress was simple enough, but on her, it looked like something right off the runway. The deep, pine green complemented her coloring, and the long, flowing style made her look even taller than she already was. She'd gotten a pair of dressy sandals with enough of a heel to put her a few inches closer to my height, but that was where things ended. No jewelry and barely any makeup.

I couldn't take my eyes off her, not even when the hostess escorted us back to the table where my brother was waiting.

"Cai, it's good to see you again." Slade rose from his seat and held out a hand.

I shook it, resisting the urge to squeeze as his gaze shifted from me to Addison. He didn't even try to hide the admiration in those damned baby blues of his.

"Slade, this is Addison Kilar. Addison, this is my little brother, Slade."

"It's nice to meet you," she said politely.

I had to stop myself from touching her just to let Slade know where things stood, but she didn't let the handshake linger. I pulled out her chair, smiling at the pleased expression on her face. Once we were all settled, Slade ordered a cheese plate and some pear thing. I had to admit, I was surprised that this was the place he'd chosen.

"The chef here is a friend of mine," he answered my unspoken question. "I helped his daughter out of a tough spot last year."

"Slade's a DEA agent," I explained to Addison.

"It seemed like a good way to put my army training to work," he said easily. He brushed back his dark hair, leaning back in his chair with that casual grace that had always gotten him the attention of pretty much every straight woman around. Half the time, I didn't think he was even aware of it, but tonight, I didn't care.

I finally had something that was mine, and I wasn't going to let my slick brother steal her from me.

I leaned closer to Addison, letting my arm brush against hers. "If you get tired, just say the word, and we'll go back to the hotel. You shouldn't get run down."

She nodded, but the look she gave me said that she knew my comment had been meant for Slade as much as it was for her.

"Is something wrong?" Slade asked, his concern genuine enough that I couldn't be annoyed by it without being a bastard.

"I work with Cai at the CDC," she answered. "We were in Pecan Grove, and I was exposed to the infection there."

She glanced at me, giving me a warm smile that I felt all the way down to my toes. She reached over and put her hand on mine. I curled my fingers around hers, the gesture so natural that I barely realized I was doing it until it was done.

"He found a cure and saved me, along with everyone else who'd been affected." She turned her attention back to Slade but didn't pull her hand away. "You guys must be so proud of everything he's done."

After a moment's hesitation, Slade responded, "We are."

"Now," she continued with a smile, "what's your favorite dish here?"

Food was an easy enough topic of conversation that I found myself able to start relaxing. I didn't contribute much, but what I observed spoke volumes. I'd never taken the opportunity to watch my brother, and now that I was, what I realized surprised me.

Under that laid-back veneer was an edge almost as sharp as the one I felt in myself. Slade had always been the funny brother, the one who eased tensions between the rest of us, the diplomat and peacemaker. He'd been that way before our parents had died – or at least as much as a five-year-old could be – but I wondered now how much of him was a mask.

"Have you spoken with Jax?" I asked during a lull in a discussion regarding the pros and cons of winter weather.

Slade took a drink before answering, "Not since I left Boston. You?"

"Monday evening, actually." I kept my tone casual. "I called him while I was waiting to see how everyone was going to respond to the treatment. I was having difficulty doing nothing."

"You've never struck me as the impatient type," Slade said. "Spending all those hours looking at bacteria and viruses, going over things hundreds of times."

I couldn't tell him that under normal circumstances, I was a patient person, but those hadn't exactly been normal. He'd want to know why, and with Addison sitting right next to me, I couldn't say it. Not when I was still trying to figure out what it all meant.

I shrugged and gave a half-assed answer. "Impatience can get the best of any of us."

I felt Addison's eyes on me but didn't look at her. She was far too observant.

"What did he have to say?" Slade asked, stabbing a piece of duck with his fork.

"He's building that club he talked to us about."

Slade's eyes darted toward Addison and back again.

"It's okay," I said. "She knows."

I left the explanation at that. He could make of it what he wanted, and if part of that assumption was that Addison and I were intimately involved enough for her to know about that, all for the better.

"Does that mean he got that woman to sell her bar?"

I shook my head. "You're not going to believe this."

I'D FORGOTTEN how much I'd enjoyed Slade's stories. He'd always had a knack for spinning tales that were a hundred times more elaborate than what had actually happened, but they were so good that no one ever minded that they were exaggerated.

"How have you not gotten fired?" Addison asked, her voice breathless with laughter.

Slade gave her that charming, irascible grin that had made

him one of the most popular guys in our school. "Technically, I wasn't on the clock."

"How have you not gotten arrested then?"

"He's always been good at getting out of trouble," I said wryly. "Remember that time you found a goat and set it loose in the school? What were you then, a junior? Senior? We thought for sure you were going to get arrested. Expelled at the very least. Instead, you got what, two weeks of detention?"

"A week," he corrected and gave me a strange look. "I was a senior, which meant you and Jax were already gone. How did you know about that?"

"Just because Jax and I were in college didn't mean we forgot about you and Blake."

The look on Slade's face said that was *exactly* what he'd thought had happened, and for the first time since I heard what Grandfather expected of us, I realized that he'd been right. Even though Slade and Blake had their own issues, Jax and I were the most responsible for what happened to us. We were the oldest, the ones our brothers should have been able to come to, but we'd let them down.

Slade looked away and the moment passed, but the smile he gave Addison didn't look quite as real as it had before. I'd never seen it before, how Slade had used his charm and humor to placate and deflect, not just between family members, but also to keep his own thoughts and feelings hidden.

He steered the conversation away from family, and I let him. I wanted to know more about his life beyond the surface things that he'd shared in Boston, and not pressuring him about the past was the best way to do it. He wasn't ready and forcing him to talk about those things would only push him away more.

As we said our goodbyes, and Addison and I rode back to the hotel, something registered so deeply within me that I knew it had to be true. That if I didn't follow the path it showed me, I'd regret it.

I needed to make amends with my brothers, starting with Jax.

It seemed Grandfather would be able to dictate his will for me after all.

TWENTY-FOUR
ADDISON

CAI WAS QUIET ON THE WAY BACK TO THE HOTEL, AND THAT in and of itself wasn't necessarily unusual, but my gut told me that this was different. This had more to do with the handsome young man we'd left back in El Paso than it did with personality. I wanted to ask him about it, but despite everything that'd happened between us, I didn't think we were at a point in our... whatever this was...for it to be okay for me to get involved.

I could, however, make sure that he knew I was here if he needed me.

As we walked into the lobby, a rather nervous-looking man approached. "Dr. Hunter, I'm glad I caught you."

Even though he'd only spoken to Cai, I stopped as well.

"Is something wrong?"

"Yes, sir." He looked like he would've been wringing his hands if it wouldn't have been unprofessional. "I'm afraid there's a problem with your room."

I'd completely forgotten that he'd booked his own room since he'd barely spent any time in it.

"A pipe burst. Your luggage, fortunately, wasn't anywhere near it, but you won't be able to stay there tonight."

"As long as there wasn't any damage to anything, there's no problem," Cai said. "We're leaving tomorrow. I can move to another room for the night."

"That's just it, Dr. Hunter. We don't have any additional rooms available. We usually keep two rooms reserved for emergencies, but one of those was also affected by the burst pipe, and the other was taken about an hour before the incident."

This was something I *could* help him with. "It's okay," I said with a smile. "We can share a room."

The man's cheeks flushed, and I wondered how long he'd been working here. If he became that embarrassed when there was no reason for him to think I was anything other than a colleague offering some space on the floor or in a chair, he'd never be able to survive the moment when a sixty-year-old man came in with a twenty-five-year-old prostitute.

"She's right," Cai said quickly. "We can share. Do you have the things from my room?"

"Yes, sir. Would you like me to have them brought up to the young lady's room?"

Cai shook his head. "I'll take them."

"Yes, sir." He scurried off, looking, in my mind, very much like the White Rabbit from *Alice in Wonderland*.

"'I'm late for a very important date,'" I murmured.

He gave me a funny look. "What was that?"

"Doesn't he remind you of the White Rabbit?"

It took Cai a moment to get it, but when he did, he laughed, and I felt some of the tension in him ease. He brushed off the apologies the manager offered, giving the man a polite smile before taking his things and walking with me to the elevator.

When the doors closed, Cai glanced down at me. "I'll call down for an extra pillow and blanket."

I was genuinely surprised. "Why?"

"They'll make the chair more comfortable."

"You don't have to sleep in the chair," I said, hoping my voice sounded more casual to Cai than it did to me.

"Addison," he said slowly, "what are you saying?"

I reached over and took his hand. "We're going home tomorrow, and whatever this is between us...with work...with our separate lives...let's give ourselves tonight. No thinking about the future, or what this means. Just tonight."

For a moment, I thought he'd refuse, tell me that this had been a huge mistake. Then the doors opened, and he leaned down to brush a kiss across the top of my head.

"I'd like that very much."

I LET out a sigh of relief as I pulled the bobby pins out of my hair. My curls tended to get a little wild, but I'd wanted them to look a little sleeker than usual for our dinner, so I'd taken the time to pin them. Now, I shook them out, letting them tumble over my shoulders, then rubbed my fingers against my scalp.

"Why didn't you wear your hair like that tonight?"

I gasped, my hand going to my chest. "You startled me."

"Sorry," Cai said with a smile. He came into the bathroom, stopping behind me. He met my eyes in the mirror. "You have beautiful hair."

I flushed. "Thank you."

He reached out and let a curl coil around his finger. "Maybe it's a good thing you didn't wear it down." He stepped closer. "Don't misunderstand me. You were beautiful in that dress and with your hair, but I don't think I would have liked it very much if Slade had gotten to see you like this."

A thrill went through me at what he said, how he said it. He had a great voice normally, but when we were like this, it dropped to something that felt like warm honey coating my skin...but without the uncomfortable stickiness.

"When you said that we could have tonight," he continued, "I don't want to make any assumption about what you meant."

"Then let me make myself clear." I leaned back against his chest. "I want whatever you're willing to give me tonight."

His eyes darkened, the intensity of those blue depths making my knees weak. "You don't know what you're asking, Little Red."

He was one of the few people who could call me 'little' and not be ironic about it. I liked it.

I smiled at him as I reached over to the side zipper of my dress. I unzipped it without looking away from him, waiting until it was down all the way until I spoke again. "I know exactly what I'm asking for...Sir."

He growled and grabbed my hair, yanking my head back and twisting it so he could claim my mouth. And that's what it felt like. Claiming. His tongue sweeping between my lips to explore. Teeth biting my bottom lip, then the top, before pulling it into his mouth to soothe it with lips and tongue.

He wasn't touching me anywhere except my hair and my mouth, but my body hummed nonetheless. It was a deep, thorough kiss, and by the time he broke contact, my breathing was ragged, and my panties were wet.

"Tell me," he demanded. "Tell me what you want me to do to you."

"Fuck me," I answered without any hesitation. "I want you to fuck me."

He smiled, but it was a dangerous sort of smile. One to which I could easily become addicted.

"Oh, I'm going to do that." He hooked his fingers under the straps of my dress. "Tell me more."

Butterflies took flight in my stomach. I trusted him, but the thought of sharing fantasies, desires, that I'd never told anyone else about, made me more nervous than I'd ever been before.

He put his mouth next to my ear. "What is it that you're holding back?" He slipped the straps off my shoulders and let the dress fall to the floor. "Tell me."

The air was cool against my flushed skin, but that wasn't the reason I shivered. I was going to tell him the truth. "That night at the club, I trusted Codie's assessment of you, but as soon as I saw you, something in my gut told me that you could be trusted. And every moment since then I've trusted you."

He swept my hair over my shoulder and kissed the place where shoulder met neck. "Ask me. Whatever it is you want, ask me."

"I want you to fuck me...bare." As the last word came out, I sought his expression in the mirror. "I've been on the pill for years, and you know I'm clean. If you tell me you are too, I trust you."

"Addison," he breathed my name as he leaned around me. His hand caught my chin, turning me until my mouth met his.

I pushed back against him, feeling his cock hardening against my ass. I slid my tongue along his, telling myself that I needed to remember every moment, that no one would ever be able to measure up to Cai.

He pulled his mouth away but rested his forehead against mine, his hand curling around my neck. "Little Red, what are you doing to me?"

I grabbed his shirt, tugging it up until I could get my hands under it and feel the tight muscles against my palms. "I don't know," I admitted. "But I feel it too."

He pulled back so suddenly that I was afraid I'd said something wrong, but then he took off his shirt and desire replaced fear. He kicked his pants aside and gestured to me.

"Off."

My bra and panties joined my dress, and then he was behind me, his hands sliding over my hips and up my ribcage, then forward until his hands covered my breasts.

"Safe word?"

"Watson," I replied promptly.

"That's a good girl," he said as he kissed the side of my neck. "Don't hesitate to use it if you want me to stop."

I nodded. "What do I say if I want you to start?"

He chuckled, then pinched my nipples between fingers and thumbs. "Easy, Little Red, or I may need to punish you for defiance."

I smiled up at him. "If you think this is defiance, I may need to show you what that word truly means."

Cai went completely still. "That mouth of yours is going to get you into trouble."

"Maybe I need something in it."

The smack on my ass caught me off guard, and I let out a startled yelp.

"I'm going to fuck you," he said. "And then we're going to get in the shower, and you're going to clean off my cock with your mouth."

"Yes, please," I said, putting my hands on the sink to brace myself.

He used his knee to nudge my legs apart, and a moment later, his cock was pushing inside me. He eased his way in, allowing me to savor how it felt to have skin against skin, nothing between us. We weren't in a relationship, but it somehow felt right that this man shared another one of my firsts, this intimate moment that required so much trust.

I groaned as he bottomed out, every thick inch of him sheathed inside me. My eyes closed, and my head fell forward, but he wasn't having that. He used my hair to yank my head up.

"Open your eyes," he ordered. "Watch us. Watch your face as I make you come."

He kept a grip on my hair as he slid almost all the way out, then slammed his hips forward, making me cry out. He repeated the process twice and then upped his pace. Each thrust drove the air from my lungs and made spots dance in front of my eyes. This wasn't a slow build-up, or a carefully kindled flame. No, this was an assault of pleasure, taking over my nerves and cells until every inch of me felt like it was on fire.

I came without warning, screaming his name even as my legs buckled. He caught me around the waist, continuing to move in and out of me even as my muscles convulsed around his cock. Finally, as I feared I couldn't take one second more, he buried himself inside me and allowed me to come.

He clung to me as our breathing slowed and pulses returned to normal. We'd shower next, and I had no doubt he'd hold me to what he'd said. I didn't mind though. I'd gladly go to my knees in front of him if it meant I'd finally get to taste him, feel the weight of him on my tongue. I wanted nothing more than the chance to make him feel as good as he'd made me feel, and the strength of that desire should have scared me. It *would* scare me...when I allowed myself to think about it. For right now, I was going to be content with where I was, and what I had.

TWENTY-FIVE

CAI

Whenever I returned to Atlanta after being in the field, it took me a couple hours to acclimate. Working in an outbreak area was akin to living in a bubble. We had to focus on what we were doing, ignore anything that could distract us. For many of us, that meant we didn't contact people back home, didn't pay attention to what was happening in the world around us.

This time was different though. I'd moved from that epidemic bubble to having two days with Addison where it was just me and her. Except for our dinner with my brother, of course, but even that had worked to bring Addison and me closer.

Now, we were on a plane, flying back to Atlanta where we would return to being intern and supervisor. We wouldn't spend time together outside of work. There'd be no repeat of the things we'd done in Texas. No more kissing, tasting, touching. I wouldn't feel the heat of her mouth on my cock like I had in the shower. Wouldn't watch her take me as far into her mouth as she could, sucking and licking until I spilled onto her tongue. I wouldn't make her come with my mouth or slide into that tight pussy of hers. And I'd never have new experiences with her, teach her all the other things that could bring her pleasure.

It was torture, sitting next to her on the plane and thinking those things, but I knew I needed to do it. I had to prepare myself, set the boundaries again. I would do the right thing and never cross that line again, but it was going to be harder than I'd first anticipated.

I glanced over at Addison and couldn't deny that it was worth it. If I was given a do-over, I wouldn't hesitate to make the same choices.

As we approached Atlanta, however, I saw something that drove all thoughts of Addison from my head.

It was snowing.

I could hardly believe my eyes. It was nothing like what I'd seen as a kid in Boston, but for Georgia, it was astounding. Fat, white flakes lazily floating to the ground where they, inexplicably, stuck.

As we got off the plane, we had to duck our heads against the snow and wind, hurrying to get to the taxi that was already waiting for us. By the time we deposited our bags in the back and climbed into the backseat, we were both shivering.

"What the hell?" Addison stammered, her teeth chattering. "Back home, this wouldn't be more than a flurry, but I thought this didn't happen down here."

"It doesn't," I said, rubbing my hands together to warm them. "I should've checked the weather report before we left."

"It wouldn't have done any good," she pointed out. "It's not like we had coats in Texas."

"Good point," I agreed.

I couldn't take seeing her shiver like that. I wrapped an arm around her and pulled her against me. "Sharing body heat," I said by way of an explanation.

She nodded, and I wasn't sure she believed my motives any more than I did.

"You ever seen shit like this before?" The cabbie leaned over the steering wheel. "I lived here my whole life and ain't never seen it snow like this before. It's actually sticking to the road."

He swerved alarmingly, and I tightened my hold on Addison. "I don't care how slow you have to go. Just get us there in one piece," I said. I lowered my voice so only Addison could hear me. "And I thought Northerners forgot how to drive during the first snow of the year."

She laughed, tucking her fingers against my side to warm them. "You think we should offer to take over? I got my license during the worst February in Minnesota history, so I started driving on worse than this."

The cab skidded, and the driver cursed. He gripped the steering wheel hard enough to turn his knuckles white, his elbows out in what would have been a comical manner if I hadn't been worried he was going to wreck. By the time we reached my place, I knew I couldn't let Addison go off with this guy, especially not on her own.

"I think you should stay with me," I said. She looked at me, surprise on her face. "We might know how to drive in this, but no one else does. It's too dangerous for you to be out. Besides, everything's going to be closed today, if it isn't already."

She looked through the windshield at the snow, and then at the clearly flustered driver. "All right. But I'll need to call Dorly, so she doesn't worry about me. And as soon as the weather clears up, I'll go home."

"Agreed."

I meant it. I was worried about her safety, and once the roads were clear again, I'd have no objection to her leaving.

Maybe if I spent the day telling myself that, I'd believe it by the time she left.

TWENTY-SIX
ADDISON

"What are you doing?"

I turned to see Cai standing behind me, holding two mugs of something with steam curling up into the cool air. He held one out to me, and I saw, with some surprise, that it was cocoa.

"Thank you," I said before answering his question. "I was taking pictures."

"Of what?" he asked as he sat down on his couch.

"The snow. My older sister, Lottie, won't believe that this little bit of snow could cause an entire city to shut down." I sat on the other side of the couch, but it was small enough that there were only a few inches between us.

"Does – *did* she live close to you?" He sipped some of the cocoa, licking his top lip to catch some of the extra foam that was stuck there.

I nodded and tried to pretend that I wasn't distracted by his mouth. "She and her family live just a few blocks over from our parents. Simon has a place in Minneapolis that's close to his son. Gene and his girlfriend got a place a few months back that's on the other side of town."

I took a drink of the cocoa and swallowed a moan. It tasted *that* good. "Was it weird for you, going from having three brothers around all the time to it being only you?"

He looked away from me, a distant expression on his face. "I'm grateful to my grandparents for what they did, taking my brothers and me, and I loved them, don't get me wrong, but I lost my family more than twenty years ago."

I reached over the small distance between us and put my hand on his arm. "I'm sorry."

"Like I said, it was more than twenty years ago."

I leaned toward him, waiting until he looked at me before I spoke, "That doesn't mean you can't still be grieving for them."

He put his hand over mine. "Thank you."

I leaned back, taking my hand with me. I picked up the mug again and busied myself with drinking it before it got cold.

After a minute or so of us drinking in silence, he broke it. "May I ask you something that's a bit personal?"

I smiled. "After everything that's happened between us, I think pretty much nothing you ask will be too personal."

"Good point." He turned so that he was angled toward me. "Why did you decide to lose your virginity to a stranger at a club?"

I shifted in my seat, wondering what had prompted him to ask that now. "I wanted something uncomplicated. No romantic entanglements. No fumbling or apologies. Codie's suggestion promised all that. It seemed like a good way to get it taken care of before it became overly awkward."

"Overly awkward?" he echoed.

"Going through high school as a virgin wasn't a big deal. And for a woman, being a virgin in college wasn't really *that* strange, especially since I was working on a Ph.D. People tend to accept academics as a legitimate reason for not having sex. But there seems to be an unspoken rule regarding virginity and age. For men, it's younger than women, but it exists for us too." I put down my now-empty mug. "A woman in her early to mid-twenties who has a religious reason for waiting to have sex – or something similar, anyway – is maybe eccentric, but it's acceptable. Someone who isn't waiting for marriage or true love, when she hits that mid-twenties mark, if she's still a virgin, it becomes all about being an ice queen. Or a lesbian – don't even get me started on that one. Or she's stuck up and doesn't think any man's good enough for her."

"People are idiots," Cai said.

I laughed. "That is definitely true. But I didn't do it for people. I didn't want it hanging over my head. And it just felt like it was time."

I was telling the truth, but I realized just then that I *did* care what Cai thought. And I didn't want him to think less of me.

"I did it for myself, not anyone else. It's what I wanted to do, and how I wanted to do it."

Cai reached out and took my hand, threading his fingers through mine. "You don't need to convince me. I believe you."

He was still holding my hand, his thumb moving over my knuckles in an almost absent manner. Little sparks of electricity danced across my skin, and the warmth that spread through my body had little to do with the cocoa and everything to do with his touch.

"Is it my turn to ask something a little personal?"

"I'm an open book," he said with a smile.

"You told me how you got involved in BDSM," I said, looking down at our linked hands. "Now, I'd like to know more about that world. I've seen some, and I know a little, but I'd like to know more."

He hooked a finger under my chin and lifted my head until our eyes met. "I'll tell you whatever you want to know, but I'd like to know why."

I reminded myself that I didn't need to be embarrassed with Cai. He'd seen me at some of the most vulnerable times of my life. "What we've done together, I know it's probably vanilla compared to what you normally do, but I liked it. A lot. And I'm wondering if it may be something I'll want to explore more."

TWENTY-SEVEN
CAI

I COULDN'T DO THIS. I DIDN'T *WANT* TO DO IT.

I thought sleeping with her in Texas would get her out of my system. That once I had her while knowing it was her, I wouldn't want her anymore. I'd never wanted any woman for more than a single night. Two nights in a row, falling asleep next to her. Both things I hadn't done before. That should have been it.

But it wasn't enough. From the moment I suggested she stay with me, I'd known I would have to face the truth of the matter sometime. I did want her to be safe and being on the roads right now definitely wasn't safe, but my desires were far less unselfish than they should have been.

Now, she was asking me to tell her about the BDSM world because she might want to explore it. We were back in Atlanta, which should have meant we had returned to intern and supervisor, but that wasn't the sort of things colleagues should discuss. And what I was thinking *definitely* wasn't something that fit into the roles we were supposed to be filling.

Damn it all to hell.

I stood and pulled her to her feet. "If I'm going to teach you, it'll be easier with visual aids."

She gave me a strange look. "We're not going to watch porn together, are we?"

I laughed. "No, Little Red, I'm going to take you to my playroom."

The nickname slipped out. I wasn't entirely sure where it had come from before, but she hadn't protested it, and now it looked like it was going to stick.

"Your playroom." The words were faint, and I could see trepidation on her face.

"Relax," I said with a smile. "Visual aids only."

Unless she wanted a more...hands-on approach. I wouldn't be able to refuse her if she asked for practical applications.

I led her down the hall to the room across from my bedroom. My apartment wasn't large, but the second bedroom was almost as big as the first, and over the years since I'd moved in, I'd filled it with all my favorite toys. I rarely ever brought women back here, which meant I hadn't had the opportunity to use it much, but it wasn't until now that I thought to ask why I'd spent the money when I didn't have a regular sub.

Maybe it was time to change that.

I glanced at Addison as I opened the door, but she looked relaxed and curious. What would she do, I wondered, if I posed the question? She seemed open to the lifestyle, and I already knew we were sexually compatible. Hell, we were sexually *explosive*. And being with her was easy. If only we didn't work together. But I was starting to think that perhaps the two of us could separate work from pleasure.

"Within the BDSM world, there are many different facets," I explained. "Exhibitionists, voyeurs, sadists, masochists, dominants, submissives, and switches."

"Switches?"

"Some people like to both dominate and sub." When she gave me a look, I shook my head. "I like my control too much to sub."

"Not surprising," she said with a smile. "I like being in control, but there's something appealing about not having to be the one making all the decisions. It lets me empty my head."

I'd wondered if submitting all the time would be a problem for her, but apparently not.

I walked over to the wall where a variety of scarves and ropes and cuffs hung. "I like bondage. Controlling how much the sub can move."

"I remember." Her lips parted as her breathing increased. "The belt."

"Restraining a sub makes it possible to push limits beyond what a sub might think they can handle. Seeing how long I can keep a sub on the edge without coming. Or the opposite, making a sub come so many times that the pleasure borders on pain."

She swallowed hard, her tongue darting out to wet her bottom lip.

"I'm not into the typical forms of punishment," I continued my explanation but took a step toward her rather than going over to the small dresser that held more of my toys. "I have a flogger, but that's it, and I rarely do anything more than a mild spanking."

She nodded. "I like that. I don't think I'd want to be whipped or anything like that." Her gaze dropped to my hands. "But a spanking..."

My jeans instantly became too tight.

"What else?" she asked softly.

"Also along the pain line, there's various forms of sensation play. Ice, wax, feathers, and the like. Sometimes I use them, but I don't generally go to the extreme with any of them."

Addison took a step toward me, and I felt like the temperature went up ten degrees.

"Then you have some other toys. Dildos, butt plugs, anal beads, gag balls." I listed off a few. "I don't really use the gag too much, but the others are quite *useful* when it comes to orgasm denial, or other sorts of...torture. That's where I like to push limits."

Her pupils were wide, with only thin slivers of pale green encircling them.

"I also like to use them for double penetration. I would never deny a sub that unique sensation, but I don't share."

"That's good," she said. "I wouldn't want to be shared."

"Any man who even considered sharing you would have to be the dumbest man alive." I cupped her cheek, my thumb brushing the side of her mouth.

I couldn't do it. I couldn't go back to the way things had been. Not knowing that someone else would take my place. Another man would truly teach her about the aspects of BDSM that appealed to her. He would be her first in other ways. He would get to hear her beg for release or sob when the sensations became too overwhelming.

And all I would have would be memories.

I was grateful for them, but I couldn't let them be the only ones I'd ever have.

I had to ask. I'd accept her decision, but if I didn't ask, I'd regret it.

"Little Red," I deliberately used the nickname, "I have a... proposition for you."

She reached up and trailed her fingers along my jaw. "Yes?"

"I know that we agreed that when we got back home, things would return to the way they had been, but now, I'm rethinking that decision." I dropped my hand from her face and caught her hand with mine. "Neither of us want something complicated, and I think we're both logical, intelligent people. We can keep things from becoming emotional."

"Just ask, Cai."

I smiled, even though my heart was pounding in my chest. "Would you be interested in an exclusive but purely physical relationship?"

"Purely physical?" she repeated.

"Our work relationship and friendship would stay the same, but we'd add sex to the mix."

"All right," she said, a grin curving her mouth. "And you said exclusive?"

I nodded, telling myself not to get too hopeful. She hadn't agreed yet. "Neither of us would become sexually involved with anyone else as long as we're sleeping together, allowing us to continue being able to forgo condoms. If that's something you'd want."

"And what if we met someone else we'd like to have sex with?" Her words were matter-of-fact, and I hoped she was simply thinking through the possibilities. I didn't like the thought that she could already want to find someone else.

"We would keep open communication," I said. "When one of us wishes to end the arrangement, we tell the other, and that is that."

She was quiet for a few minutes, and I wished I could hear what she was thinking. I'd put myself out there, asking her this, but if she agreed, it would be well worth it.

Finally, she nodded. "That would work for me."

I leaned down and took her mouth in a hard, possessive kiss. She was mine. I didn't know for how long, but I intended to make the most of every second we were together. I would leave my mark on her so deep that I would be the standard by which every other man would be measured.

No. I wouldn't think of other men. She would only be with

me. I had so much to teach her, and we would begin tonight. Until we parted ways, she was mine, and that was what mattered.

Mine.

TWENTY-EIGHT

ADDISON

THIS WAS...DIFFERENT.

I was naked – that wasn't the different part – and I was on the bed, face-down. My wrists were tied to each other, and to each ankle, pulling my legs out and up. The position also kept my arms up, parallel to my back. He'd had me braid my hair, then tied the bottom of my braid to the restraints around my wrist. My head was pulled back, stretched right to the very edge of comfort. I was pretty sure adrenaline had something to do with the fact that I wasn't uncomfortable yet, but I'd take it. I didn't want to be in a position where I'd need to use my safe word. The thought of disappointing Cai bothered me in a way in which I wasn't accustomed.

My head was at the bottom of the bed, so I was able to see Cai as he stopped in front of me. He'd removed his clothing as well, giving me a heart-stopping view of strong thighs, those deep v-grooves at his hips, and a thick, full erection.

"I let you take control the first time, but now, it's my turn."

He put his hand on the back of my head, not exerting any pressure, but rather providing a reminder that he was in charge.

As if I could forget it.

"Open."

I parted my lips, eager anticipation coiling in my belly. He slid his cock into my mouth, taking it slow. The taste of him exploded across my tongue, and I licked around him, savoring the texture as well. The skin was soft, delicate, but the muscle beneath it was firm. He made a few shallow thrusts before speaking.

"Are you able to snap your fingers?"

I snapped my fingers in response.

"That will be your safety sound if you're not able to use your safe word," he explained. "Snap again if you understand."

I did as he asked, and he rewarded me by inching forward until he was almost at the back of my throat. A flutter of panic unfolded in my chest, but I pushed it down. I trusted him not to take things too far, to know where my limits were, even if I didn't know them myself.

As he began to pull back, I applied suction, remembering that he'd enjoyed that before. I earned the same moan as before and dedicated myself to making him feel even better. I tried to move my head to control the depth of his strokes, but a jolt of pain in my scalp reminded me why that wasn't a good idea.

"Stay where you are." Cai sounded amused. "I'll take care of things from my end."

I responded by flicking my tongue across the tip of his cock, then teasing the slit before he could push deeper. My muscles began to ache, unused to being in this position, but I didn't stop. I'd never been the sort of person who cared about what other people thought, but with this, I found that Cai's opinion was important to me.

"Fuck, Little Red, that mouth..."

I'd take that as a positive endorsement.

"I'm close," he warned. "If you don't want me to come in your mouth, snap your fingers twice."

I clenched my hands into fists, so he couldn't even mistake me wanting him to stop. His fingers dug into my hair, his hips jerking as he lost his rhythm. For a moment, he almost went too far, but then he was sliding back enough to coat my tongue with his seed. I swallowed, sucking as hard as I could, wanting to draw out every last drop.

He curled over me, his breathing ragged, and kissed the top of my head. "Thank you, Little Red."

I hadn't been sure about that nickname when he first used it, but the more I heard it, the more it grew on me.

He straightened, his cock slipping from my mouth. He hadn't gone completely soft, and I knew he'd be ready again soon. His fingers moved behind me, and the tension holding my head in place disappeared. My scalp throbbed, and I breathed a sigh of relief.

"How are your arms and legs?" Cai asked as he pulled apart the braid with surprising gentleness. "Circulation good? Muscles?"

I flexed my fingers, testing them even as I rolled my ankles, wiggled my toes. "Circulation's fine, but my muscles are starting to feel it."

He gave me a searching look. "Five more minutes."

I nodded. Having my head free made me feel my legs and arms less.

He moved around behind me, the bed shifting under me as he climbed onto it. I expected to feel his touch, but I still jumped when a fingertip traced my lips. He ran his finger between them, pushing it inside for a few quick strokes. Instead of adding a second finger, however, he withdrew it completely. A moment later, it teased over somewhere else entirely.

"Easy," he murmured as he placed a hand on the small of my back. "Just a finger tonight. Trust me."

I nodded, then put my head down, closing my eyes to shut

out everything except what Cai was doing. I sucked in a breath as the finger breached that tight ring of muscle. I knew enough about anal sex to expect the burn that followed, and I breathed through it. What I found, however, was that once I was past that, a different sort of heat was spreading through me. I'd been turned on already, and the sensations combined for something even more intense than I felt before. Not *better*, necessarily, but different.

"I'm going to release your legs in a moment," Cai said. "But unless you say the word, your hands will remain as they are."

"Yes, Sir," I said, trying to keep the relief from my voice. I was in good shape, but this wasn't exactly a normal exercise.

His finger disappeared, and then the tie between my hands and feet was gone too, allowing my hands to fall to my back, and my feet to the bed. I waited for Cai to turn me over, unable to do it myself with my hands as they were, but that wasn't what happened.

He grasped my hips and pulled me up onto my knees, leaving me to catch my weight on my chest and shoulders. I wasn't given long to process it though because he drove into me with one solid thrust, and suddenly, that was all I could feel...think...know.

My world expanded and contracted with every stroke. The heat of his hands on my hips was nothing compared to the fire he was stoking inside me. Nerves fired over and over, transmitting signals of pleasure and pain one right after the other. My legs had begun to protest, and my fingertips were tingling, but none of it was enough to make me want him to stop. The pressure inside me had built too far for much of anything to distract me.

Then, suddenly, his cock moved against that spot inside me and the world exploded in a blast of pleasure and light. But it didn't stop there. As Cai continued at his bruising, brutal pace, one orgasm rolled into another until I finally realized what he'd meant about coming too many times. I was almost at that point, but before I tipped over that edge, Cai groaned my name, his cock pulsing inside me as he climaxed.

Neither one of us spoke as we slumped onto the bed, a tangle of sweat-slicked limbs. He untied my hands after a minute, wrapping his arms around me so he could massage my hands and wrists. The silence between us was comfortable and familiar, as if we'd been lovers for years.

We wouldn't ever be that, I knew. We weren't in a relationship. We could refer to each other as lovers, but we weren't in love. Ours was an agreement based on sexual compatibility, respect, and the fact that we got along with each other so well. I was confident that we would be able to amicably part ways when the time came.

But as Cai pulled the blanket over us, I couldn't help but wonder if he was going to get tired of me before I was ready to let him go.

TWENTY-NINE

CAI

I'D ALWAYS AVOIDED VALENTINE'S DAY AT ALL COSTS, never wanting anyone to feel as if I was either taking advantage of them or reading more into things than was there. I hadn't, however, thought twice about sleeping with Addison on Valentine's Day. I trusted that she would see it for what it was, and nothing more.

We'd only been 'snowed in' that one night, but after having spent so much time together, it had been strange when she'd gone back to her place, leaving me completely alone for the first time since we left for Texas. I'd been worried that, once we'd been apart for a couple days, we'd see each other at work and things would be awkward.

But they weren't.

We got along just as well as we had before. The only awkward moment had come when Dr. Edison had come into the lab looking for Pansy, and I'd had to explain why she wasn't there. At least the paperwork I possessed to prove that Addison had indeed been infected supported my decision to send her back to Atlanta and alert Dr. Fenster that I'd taken it upon myself to fire Pansy. He'd backed me up without question, trusting my judgment, but having the evidence to back it up made me feel better.

He'd also made sure security had escorted her to her desk, waited while she'd packed up her things, and then escorted her out. Rumor had it, she'd cussed them out non-stop. She'd left a few nasty voicemails and sent a couple vicious texts, but I'd blocked her number, and that had been that.

Addison and I had spent a few hours together Wednesday night, where I taught her a little bit about orgasm denial. I didn't, however, tell her that spending nearly forty-five minutes teasing her with my mouth, my fingers, and a vibrator had tortured me as much as it had her.

Yesterday, I'd asked her to join me at the club where we'd met before, but this time as an official date. Well, not a 'date' in the sense of us defining what we were doing as dating, but just as us going somewhere together.

I was aware, every time I thought of this, that I was simply making excuses, and I needed to accept the fact that I wanted us to have a more solid definition of who we were to each other. I refused to dwell on it, however, knowing that if I changed anything, I could lose Addison entirely, and I wasn't willing to risk that.

Besides, I didn't want a relationship with her. I just didn't want anyone else to have her. We'd agreed to be monogamous, and I'd been telling the truth when I said that it was so that we didn't have to return to using condoms, but I couldn't deny the jealousy I felt at the idea of her with another man.

Tonight, however, I would walk into the club with her on my arm, and it would be clear to everyone there that she was off-limits.

I gave her another sideways glance as she smoothed down her skirt. I'd picked her up rather than having her meet me since I didn't want her going inside alone. The club was usually adept at keeping out the unsavory element who too often liked to take advantage of new people looking into the BDSM lifestyle, but I didn't trust anyone else to keep Addison safe, especially not after I learned her friends, Dorly and Codie, wouldn't be there.

"Are you certain you're comfortable coming back here?" I asked. "Going here isn't something I feel strongly that I need. I don't have a personal connection, I mean."

She reached over and took my hand. "I'm curious," she admitted. "I think I'll be able to see it through different eyes than I had before. Plus, it's at least one place where the chances of running into someone from work are slim."

"I agree." I squeezed her hand, hoping she'd understand that I wasn't ashamed of her or anything like that. Work finding out about us was a headache that neither of us needed.

My heart was thudding as we pulled into the parking garage next to the club. I'd never been nervous coming in here before, but this would be the first time I'd come with someone aside from that first time.

I had a sudden, sinking feeling that my choice to let her in would come back to bite me in the ass.

I stepped around to her side of the car but wasn't quick enough to get the door for her. Still, I offered her my hand and helped her get out. I didn't release her as we walked away, but rather pulling her closer, so I could tuck her hand around my arm.

"Remember, if you want to leave, just say the word," I said as we approached the door.

She nodded, then stretched up to kiss my cheek. "Relax. Everything's going to be fine."

I smiled, but I knew I wouldn't relax until I saw how comfortable she was.

We stayed near the edges of the Friday night crowd, but before too long, she pulled me onto the dance floor. I tried to protest, but then she'd given me a mischievous smile, and I knew she'd done it on purpose, wanting to push my own limits.

I was nothing if not up for a challenge.

It took me a minute to find the rhythm, but when I stopped trying to follow the music, and instead followed Addison, it came easily. I reached out and put my hands on her hips, drawing her to me. In my peripheral vision, I saw more than a few people watching us, but I didn't give them anything more than cursory attention. I wasn't here for them.

She reached up and put her hands on my shoulders, sliding them across, and then up around my neck. We had a few inches between our bodies, but that didn't stop the electricity that flowed back and forth.

The music was background noise, the lights a mere backdrop. We moved together as if we'd been doing it for years. I'd never enjoyed dancing because I'd never really been in sync with someone, but Addison and I had some sort of instinct when it came to each other. When the song changed, our rhythm matched it, both of us adapting at the same time without a word said.

Something about being with her had altered me in some deeply profound way that I didn't fully understand yet. I'd always accepted my sexual preferences as a part of who I was, but it wasn't until now that being here felt natural. This was something I wanted. A place to go where the two of us could be who we were and no one would judge.

And then it hit me. *This* was what Jax wanted, the reason why he'd continued to look for ways to build his club even after Grandfather had told him that it wasn't something Hunter Enterprises should get into. The club that Jax built would be better than this one. He hadn't told me any of his plans, but I knew my brother well enough to know that he wouldn't be satisfied with anything less than perfection.

I needed to call him and tell him that I understood now. But that wasn't the only reason why. I was tired of ignoring the issues between us. Having dinner with Slade had made me realize that, no matter how many times I said that I enjoyed being alone, I missed my brothers. What happened to us should have brought us together, but instead, it'd torn us apart. Grandfather had wanted us to mend our relationships, even if he'd gone about it in a less-than-orthodox manner.

Slade wasn't ready yet, and I had a feeling Blake would be the hardest to reach, but my most recent conversation with Jax made me think that things could start with us.

THIRTY
ADDISON

CAI HAD A LOT GOING ON IN HIS HEAD, AND WHILE A PART of me wished he'd only be here with me, in this moment, I knew that wasn't something I could ask of him. We'd agreed to sex, and that was somewhere I could ask for his full attention, but anything else was extra.

Besides, I would've been lying if I'd said other things weren't catching my eye. When I'd come before, I hadn't been prepared for it. Tonight, however, I saw things through different eyes. I looked past the clothes and looked for the people. I began to categorize them as Doms and subs, mentally filing away things like collars and leashes; if they walked side-by-side or one trailed behind. I knew that not everyone fit into nice little boxes, but these lists and commonalities – finding patterns – helped me understand, and that was ultimately what I wanted to do.

"What are you thinking?"

Cai's voice barely carried over the music, and I took a step closer to him before answering, "I'm finding the patterns."

He nodded, and I could see in his eyes that he wasn't trying to placate me. He understood exactly what I meant. His hands slid around my hips to my ass, and he pulled me tight against him.

"Would you like to check out one of the rooms?"

Like I'd ever turn down sex with Cai. I nodded eagerly, placing my hand in his, and then following him over to a sign in sheet. We filled it out, checked the appropriate boxes and then headed to the closest empty room.

It wasn't the same room we'd been in the last time, but I was glad to see that it wasn't a chains and leather dungeon, but rather a tastefully decorated room. It wasn't over-the-top lavish, but it wasn't the sort of place that made me feel like I was in a cheap porn either. A bed and a few chairs were the only pieces of furniture, but the walls held a dozen different toys, some of which I recognized from Cai's playroom. The color scheme was red and gold, and for a moment, my mind immediately thought of *Harry Potter*, making me laugh.

Cai gave me a sideways look. "Not exactly the response I'd been going for."

"I couldn't help it," I admitted. "I saw the colors and thought 'X-rated Gryffindor common room.'"

For a moment, he stared at me, and then he burst into laughter. He pulled me to him and wrapped his arms around me in a tight embrace. I buried my face in his chest, and his scent surrounded me. He kissed the top of my head, and I thought that I could be happy right here, with him, this way.

"I have a confession to make," he said as he released me. "I've always had a thing for Ginny Weasley."

I rolled my eyes and shook my head, laughing along with him. "I'll never be able to watch those movies the same way again."

He raised my hand and brushed his mouth against my knuckles. "There's something I want you to do for me, Little Red."

The mood in the room shifted instantly.

"What is it?" I asked, my stomach clenching in anticipation.

"Have a seat." He gestured to a simple wooden chair that sat at the foot of a double bed.

I sat on the edge, unsure of where he was going to take this.

"Are you wearing a bra?"

I flushed despite the fact he'd already seen me naked more than once. "No."

"Panties?"

"Yes."

"Pull down your top until your breasts are exposed."

Somehow, the matter-of-fact way he gave the order made it that much hotter. He folded his arms across his chest and watched as I slipped the straps from my shoulders and tugged at the top until the neckline was under my breasts.

"Scoot back." After I did, he gave another command. "Spread your legs as wide as is comfortable. Pull up the skirt if necessary."

The dull thudding of the music from the other side of the door was nothing compared to my heart slamming into my ribs.

"I'm going to watch you masturbate," he said, pulling another chair into the middle of the room. When it was directly opposite me, he sat, his posture laid-back, even if the vibe in the room was anything but. "Make yourself come for me, Little Red."

Somehow, being exposed the way I was, with him fully dressed, made the Dom / sub dynamic of our relationship clearer than ever, and I found that I wasn't simply curious about it. I liked it.

A lot.

I knew enough about this sort of thing to know that meeting Cai's gaze wasn't what a good sub would do, but I'd never agreed to be *good*.

When my eyes met his, he didn't scold me. He didn't say a word at all. He simply raised an eyebrow, as if he had nothing else to do but wait for me to obey.

I pulled my skirt higher, then dropped my hand between my legs. The crotch of my panties was wet, but that didn't surprise me. *Not* being aroused when I was around Cai was unusual.

The first touch made me shiver. Despite having been a virgin until recently, I hadn't been inhibited when it came to my sexuality. I'd tried different things, discovered the ways I could bring myself to climax quickly, as well as the things I could do to draw things out.

I pushed aside the damp fabric and traced my lips until Cai's attention fell, and I knew he was ready to watch. One finger slipped between, gathered moisture, then teased the tip of my clit. A light tingle danced down my nerves, and I started with small circles, easing my body into what was to come.

A second finger joined the first, and I made a V shape, rubbing either side of my clit as it swelled and throbbed. I moved my hand lower, my palm pressing down as I slid my fingers inside me. The combination of sensations made me close my eyes, and I let my head fall back.

Faster and faster. More pressure, taking me almost to pain. Slick skin against skin. Up, down, around. Alternating motions to take me closer to release.

And all the while, I was aware of Cai watching me. He didn't speak, but it wasn't sound that told me he was still near. I felt him, the weight of his gaze, the heat, and the energy pulsing off him.

I wanted to come for myself, but I also wanted to do it for him. My orgasm was no longer for me alone.

My muscles tightened, and a spike of pain and pleasure shot through me. I pulled up my legs without even thinking about it, my body curling forward, as if I could contain an explosion by wrapping my body around me. Then I was there, limbs shaking, breath coming out in gasps.

As the ecstasy faded, my muscles unclenched, and I flopped back into the chair, uncaring that my legs were splayed wide, my breasts still exposed.

A strange rattling sound made me open my eyes a minute or so later. Cai had returned his chair to its place against the wall, and now he was pressing a button. I couldn't figure out what he was doing until I followed his gaze up to the ceiling and watched a pair of chains descend. On the end of each one was a metal cuff.

I had a good idea what Cai wanted to do next.

Shit.

"Are you able to stand?" He broke the silence.

"Yes," I said.

"Do it."

I stood and resisted the impulse to adjust my clothes. Being a sub was an awful lot like playing the kids' game 'Simon Says.' I'd do nothing until he told me.

No matter how uncomfortable my panties had become.

"Take off your panties."

I did, grateful to be rid of them.

"Set them on the chair, and then walk over to the chains."

He joined me a few seconds later, still completely dressed. I looked up at him as he reached out and pinched my nipple. He cupped my breasts, lightly squeezing before leaning down to take my nipple between his teeth. He tugged on it, then rubbed the tip of his tongue back and forth until I could no longer stand still. I clenched my hands into fists, shifting my weight from foot to foot.

When he straightened, the smug smile on his face told me that he'd intentionally pushed me until I had to squirm. I swallowed a smart comment, more eager to move on than I was to get into a debate. He took one hand, lifting my arm until he could latch the cuff around my wrist. Some sort of material covered the inside of it, offering some padding. Still, if he wanted to, he could make me hurt.

I trusted him, though, and said nothing as he latched the remaining cuff around my other wrist. My arms were up, but not stretched too tightly. I twisted my wrists to get a feel for the restraints but didn't try to get free.

The sound of a zipper drew my attention back to him. He still wore all his clothes, but now, his erection was free, curving up toward his stomach. He stroked it a couple times, then put his hands on my hips. He lifted me, and I pulled on the chains to balance.

"Wrap your legs around my waist," he said.

I did, his cock rubbing against me as he worked to line us up. Then he was there, sliding inside me like two pieces of a puzzle coming together. His hands locked together at the small of my back, holding me flush against his body. My torso, however, had no extra support unless I used my arms. And with him thick and pulsing inside me, I could barely remember my name, much less how to maneuver with my arms like this.

Then his mouth covered my breast, the suction hard enough to make me gasp. His teeth scraped and nipped my flesh, leaving marks, but I didn't care. Every sensation went straight to my core, mixing with the almost too-full feeling as he began to move.

I had an odd sense of weightlessness as he controlled every movement. He drove his hips up as he used his arms to pull me down, pushing him deeper than he'd ever been before. My legs were locked around his waist, but I had no illusions about who was in charge here. His mouth moved across my skin, but he didn't miss a single stroke.

This time, he came first, fingers digging into my hips as he ground me down against him, giving me that last little bit of pressure I needed to follow. Even as he emptied himself inside me, I didn't think for a moment that he would let me go. With him, I was always safe.

And I didn't want to lose that.

One day I would, I knew, and all I could do was choose to enjoy the time I had. Which meant I had to focus on the here and now. The future would take care of itself.

THIRTY-ONE

CAI

I LET OUT A SLOW BREATH AND TAPPED MY BROTHER'S name. There was no going back now. Even if he didn't answer, he'd see that I called.

"Cai? Is everything okay?" Jax's voice was more worried than I'd ever heard him. Even when he called about Grandfather, his voice had been flat, controlled.

"I'm fine," I said, sitting down in my favorite chair. It was an old thing I'd found at a garage sale, but it was far more comfortable than the most expensive piece of furniture I'd had growing up.

"Not that I'm not glad to hear from you," he said, "but you must admit, it's not exactly a normal thing. I mean, the last time you called, you were in Texas dealing with some epidemic."

I took the route he offered. "I'm back in Atlanta now, with my whole team. The treatment I came up with knocked the infection out, and we were able to locate the source and contain it. I don't know if I thanked you for helping to get my mind off things for a while but thank you."

"Are you sure you're okay?" he asked.

"I saw Slade."

Silence.

"How is he?" Jax's voice was strangely soft when he finally asked. "I've been wanting to call him and Blake to tell them about Syll, but I didn't know how they'd take it. I don't want any of you to think I'm reaching out because of Grandfather's ultimatum and what it means for my position at the company."

"Aren't you?" I was honestly curious.

"Are you?" he countered. "You've called me twice since you left Boston."

"You know I'm not interested in being a part of Hunter Enterprises. And I don't need Grandfather's money." I picked at a loose thread. "He should have just let you have it all. You're the one who followed in his footsteps."

I let my words sit as I waited for a response. I hadn't flat-out told him that I'd called because I wanted to address what was between us, but I knew him well enough to know he now understood that I was trying.

"I always admired you, Cai," he said finally. "You excelled at everything. School. Sports. You could've stepped up into Hunter Enterprises at any time and left me in the dust. But you knew what you wanted to do, and you didn't let anyone stop you."

I sat in stunned silence. He admired me?

"Grandfather was proud of you," he continued. "I know he wasn't the sort of man who talked about his feelings, but he bragged about you, all of you guys actually. Every event we hosted or attended, he'd find a way to bring up his successful grandsons. He loved telling people how you worked at the CDC, how you'd gotten there all on your own. Never asked him for help or to make a call."

"I never knew," I said softly. "I always thought he held it against me that I hadn't wanted to join you in the family business. That I'd done what Dad had done and went off to do my own thing."

"The night he...that night, he was with Ms. K, and I hadn't even realized he wasn't in the house. The two of us had lived under the same roof for years, and we rarely spoke outside of work. We never talked about anything that was really important."

Was Jax really saying that his conversations with Grandfather about work weren't important? It didn't seem possible. Hunter Enterprises meant so much to him.

Before the accident, he'd talked about being a professional golfer or a fireman – the usual dreams children had – but not long after the accident, he'd told our grandparents that he wanted to work at Hunter Enterprises. From that moment, he hadn't faltered.

"Jax, did you really *want* to run the company?"

He gave a small laugh. "I think you're the first person to ask me that. From the moment I walked into the dining room and announced to Grandfather and Grandma Olive that I wanted to work at Hunter Enterprises, everyone took it as how things would be. No one thought to ask if I'd been in the right frame of mind, or even old enough to understand what I was saying. And no one ever asked if I'd changed my mind."

"You'd sounded so sure," I said. "And you made Grandfather so happy."

"He did what he thought was best at the time," Jax said. "But in the end, even he knew that he could have done better."

"I was never able to measure up," I admitted. "You were doing everything Grandfather had wanted from Dad, doing odd jobs at the company by the time you were twelve. Everyone loved you."

"Cai," Jax began.

I didn't let him continue. I needed to get this out now, or I'd never say it. "I pushed myself because I thought if I could somehow show that I was as good as you, Grandfather would see me too."

"Shit, Cai, I didn't know."

"No one did," I said. "When I first heard those stipulations, all I could think was that it was just Grandfather trying to control us after all, force us into being just like you."

Jax laughed. "My first thought was confusion. I was so full of myself that I couldn't imagine what Grandfather had meant. We'd just grown apart like siblings do."

I'd made the call, and I was going to take the initiative. "I'm not doing this because of Grandfather's will, but I'd like to see if we can..." I searched for the words.

"Be brothers again?"

I swallowed around a sudden lump in my throat. "Yes. I'd like that."

After a moment, Jax cleared his throat. "How's your colleague?"

I appreciated the change of subject – that was enough talking about our emotions for today – and followed. "Addison is great."

"Addison?"

I ignored the question. "How's Syll?"

"She's great. You should come back soon so you can meet her before the wedding."

"You're rushing into things, aren't you?" I asked. "You've only known her for a month. An engagement is one thing. Getting married that fast is something else."

"We're thinking next year," Jax said. "But what are the chances you'll be back before then?"

He had a point. Before Grandfather's death, it'd been three years since I'd visited. As I talked to my brother, however, I couldn't imagine not seeing him for another three years.

For the first time since I'd moved to Atlanta, Boston was too far away.

"I'll plan something soon," I said.

"Maybe you can bring your *colleague*, Addison."

I could hear the smirk in his voice. "It's not like that."

"Oh, really? What's it like then?"

"She's my intern, and we spend a lot of time together. We're friends." All of that was true. Just not the whole truth.

"Do you remember that day at the cemetery when I told you guys about Syll and the club? How I didn't want to talk about her?"

I made a noise of affirmation, not liking the direction this conversation was taking.

"Syll turned my entire world upside-down," Jax said without a trace of embarrassment or sarcasm. "She made me see that I could tell myself how fulfilling my work was, and even mean it, but without family, it would never make me happy. She made me see myself in a way no one else ever had."

"I'm happy for you." The words fell flat, but not because I didn't think Jax deserved to be happy. Rather, I kept thinking about how I'd opened up to Addison more than I had anyone else in my life.

"I'm not going to pry," Jax said. "But I will say this: if she makes you want to be a better man, *and* she gives you what you need to accomplish that, don't let her go."

We made a little more small talk before ending the call, both of us promising that we would talk again soon. And it wasn't just something to say. We both meant it.

I stayed in the chair after we'd said goodbye, thinking about everything we'd said, and everything we had left to say. I'd had an idea in the back of my mind ever since I'd talked to Jax while I was in Texas. An idea that was now starting to feel more like something I *needed* to do.

If Jax and I were really going to mend things between us, and do it *right*, we couldn't do it over the phone or in weekend visits. I'd left Jax before, forcing him to carry a burden I hadn't realized he'd had. He couldn't come to me, but I could go to him.

The CDC had a branch in Boston, and Dr. Fenster had connections there.

If this had happened right after the funeral, I would've applied for a transfer without a second thought, because all I'd had here was work.

But now, I had Addison, and I wasn't sure I could leave her.

THIRTY-TWO
ADDISON

"THIS IS FABULOUS." CODIE LET OUT A MOAN THAT MADE me a little uncomfortable. "Can I marry you?"

I laughed as I leaned back in my seat. I patted my stomach, feeling delightfully full. "I think Dorly might have something to say about that."

"I don't know," Dorly countered. She scooped up the last of the peach cobbler I'd made. "For access to food like this, I'd be willing to share."

"Where did you learn to cook like this?" Codie asked. Her tongue stud clinked against her spoon as she licked the utensil clean. "Your mom?"

"No, Mom was always too busy to do more than heat up frozen dinners or bring something home." I scraped my spoon along the bottom of my bowl. "She worked full-time, and there were a lot of us kids. We all pitched in, but none of the rest of them could cook. When I was eleven or twelve, I decided to try my hand at cooking. I talked to this old woman who lived across the hall. Mrs. Dressen. She offered to teach me if I'd walk her dog, Puddles."

"I'd like to send Mrs. Dressen a thank you card," Codie said.

"Does your secret beau know you can cook like this?" Dorly asked with a sly grin. "And don't pretend you don't know what I'm talking about, because you two were top of the gossip chain at the club."

"Dammit."

"What's going on with you?" Codie asked. "I mean, you went from single virgin to dirty dancing with a tall hottie and then heading to a room with him."

I gulped down the rest of my water. I told them some of what happened in Pecan Grove, but I'd stuck with the work part of things. How I'd gotten exposed. Pansy getting fired. But I hadn't told them about what I discovered about Cai, or the arrangement we'd come to. Neither one of them knew that Cai was a gorgeous thirty-one-year-old, so when I'd mentioned that my supervisor had stayed with me. For all they knew, he was a balding, middle-aged man.

"The guy at the club was the same guy I slept with there that first time." I started with the easy part.

"Seriously?" Codie's eyes went wide. "How did you two meet up again? I mean, the likelihood of you two both showing up at the club at the same time, recognizing each other–"

I held up a hand. "That's not how it worked."

Dorly gave me a searching look. "I have a feeling this is a story."

I nodded. "It is."

"You need a beer to tell it?" she asked.

"That would be nice," I said. Alcohol wasn't called *liquid courage* for nothing.

She came back with three bottles and settled back onto the couch. She put an arm around Codie and then faced me expectantly.

"When I was in quarantine in Texas, I was talking to Dr. Hunter. He made a comment about the head of the hospital – a woman – flirting with me. I made a joke about my gaydar improving since I started spending time with you. I mentioned you both by name, and that's when Cai realized that he knew the two of you."

Both Codie and Dorly were staring at me.

"I figured it out first," I continued, "but as soon as I said the safe word he'd given me, he knew who I was."

"Wait a minute." Dorly leaned forward, eyes flashing. "Your boss fucked you?"

"Dorly!" Codie smacked her girlfriend's arm.

"Neither one of us knew who the other was," I admitted. "He told me to call him 'Sir,' and I gave him my middle name, 'May.' And, if you remember, you guys put bronze glitter in my hair so he wouldn't have even had that clue, and we both wore masks."

"Still." Dorly scowled. "It's not okay."

Heat flooded my face, and my usually dormant temper flared. "Then I guess you're really going to be pissed at me when I tell you that we've been *fucking* since Pecan Grove."

"Addison," Codie leaned forward and put her hand on my arm, "we're just worried about you. Your boss...that's not okay."

"He didn't force me or coerce me!" I snapped. "Cai's not like that."

"He's still your supervisor," Dorly said, her voice harsh. "You're an intern. Plus, you've been going on about how amazing *Dr. Hunter* is since you got here. Of course, you wouldn't see it if he was applying pressure."

"We discussed it like adults," I said, pushing myself up from my seat. I had to make them see that this wasn't a case of someone in power pressuring me to have sex with them. "Everything that happened between us was one hundred percent consensual. Cai respects me and my opinions. We're friends and co-workers first. Sex is separate."

"And what happens when one of you wants more?" Dorly asked. "Do you honestly think you'll be able to go back to working together if...*when* things end badly?"

"We agreed that when the time came, we would talk about it, and then we would end the sexual part of our relationship."

Dorly rolled her eyes. "I thought you were smarter than that. No couple breaks up and then works together like nothing ever happened."

"We aren't a couple," I said.

She raised an eyebrow. "So, you're both fucking other people?"

"No," I said, facing her, my arms crossed over my chest. "We're being monogamous by choice. If we ever want to get involved with other people, then we talk about it. We're both logical, intelligent people. Emotions beyond friendship and respect don't play a role in what we're doing."

Dorly shook her head. "You're making a huge mistake."

Codie came over to me and put her hand on my shoulder. "Addison, don't you think it's possible that he could be manipulating you? Taking advantage of your hero worship?"

"He's not like that. Come on, Codie, you're the one who thought he'd be perfect for my first time because he was a good guy."

"For an anonymous encounter, yes, but if I would've known he was your boss, I never would've suggested it."

I shook my head. "Cai is an honorable, respectful man who would never take advantage of anyone for anything. The fact that he's my supervisor doesn't change his character."

"Shit," Codie breathed, her eyes wide.

"What now?"

"You're in love with him."

"What?" I shook my head. "You're crazy. We're friends who work together and have sex. That's all there is between us."

"Addison, you need to take a good, hard look at yourself, because if you don't acknowledge how you really feel, you're going to get in way too deep, and you'll be devastated when things end." Codie wore a sympathetic expression that was somehow worse than her anger. "I know how much you value your work, and I'd hate to see you do something that would hurt everything you've worked toward."

"I'm not in love with him," I said firmly. "Hell, I don't even know if I believe in love."

"It doesn't matter if you believe in it or not," she said. "It's true, and the sooner you accept it, the better."

She was wrong. She had to be. I wouldn't have fallen in love with Cai when I knew it would only end with heartbreak. Neither one of us wanted a romantic entanglement. We'd agreed.

Work. Friends. Sex.

Nothing romantic. Nothing emotionally intimate. Freedom to leave at any time without any hurt feelings.

My text tone went off, and I turned away from Codie and Dorly to pick up my phone. It was a text from Cai.

I'd like you to go to dinner with me tonight. There are a few things I'd like for us to talk about.

He wanted to talk.

Was he ending things already, thinking that taking me out to dinner would soften the blow? Or maybe he thought that if we were in public, I'd be less likely to make a scene. How had he met someone else? Maybe he hadn't met someone. Maybe he'd just gotten tired of me. Or maybe he'd realized that sex with me wasn't worth the risk for us at work.

And that was when it hit me.

I cared.

I didn't want him to break things off with me for any reason.

I didn't care about work or what anyone else thought, for that matter.

Shit.

Codie was right.

I was in love with Cai.

THIRTY-THREE

CAI

THIS WASN'T LIKE ME AT ALL. I PLANNED THINGS OUT, carefully weighed the risks and rewards. I didn't rush headlong into things. Except that character trait of mine didn't seem to apply to Addison. I'd barely thought through a single step of our relationship, from the moment she'd run into me at work to me asking her about having an exclusive sexual relationship. All that had mattered to me was that I didn't lose her.

Talking with Jax had made two things perfectly clear to me. One, it was time to go back to Boston. Maybe not forever, but for a while. Long enough to get to know my brother again. The second thing I'd discovered was that I couldn't continue with Addison the way things were going now. We'd never been only about sex, and I needed to make sure she saw that, because I was going to do something rash.

I was going to ask her to come to Boston with me.

I tugged on my suit jacket and wondered if I should have worn a tie. I didn't own many of them and generally reserved wearing them for occasions like presentations or fundraisers. The jacket I wore only on formal occasions when it was too chilly for just a dress shirt. Tonight, felt like one of those nights clothes-wise, but I'd never been this nervous before any other social event.

Probably because my entire future had never been dependent on one person's answer to a question before.

With one hand, I held up the flowers I'd bought, and then I knocked with the other. When the door opened, however, Dorly stood there, scowling, her arms crossed.

"If you hurt Addison, I will cut off your balls and give them to her as earrings."

I blinked. "Wow. That's an oddly specific threat."

She shrugged. "I believe in fair warnings."

She stepped aside, and I walked past her. Codie was here too, perched on the arm of a loveseat. She didn't look any more pleased to see me than Dorly did.

"What Dorly said, about the earrings," Codie glared at me, "after she's done, I'll cut off your dick and feed it to a pig."

Despite the fact their threats were enough to make me want to back away with my hands over my crotch, I appreciated the fact that they cared enough about Addison to promise bodily harm if I hurt her.

"Both duly, noted." I said.

"Addison, your date's here!" Dorly called without taking her eyes off me.

"You're early," Addison said as she rushed out of what I assumed was her bedroom. She pushed curls back from her flushed face. "I need a couple minutes to get this mess under control."

I smiled at her. "Please don't. I like your hair wild."

Her cheeks grew redder, but her eyes sparkled. "Are those for me?"

I held out the flowers, and when her fingers brushed against mine, a little jolt of electricity moved up my arm. "I remembered you saying you liked sunflowers."

"They're my favorite," she said as she cradled the flowers in her arms for a moment. "Dorly, would you mind putting these in water for me?"

Dorly took the bouquet, throwing me one final dirty look before heading to the kitchenette.

"Shall we?" I asked, holding out my hand.

When Addison's fingers laced between mine, I knew I had to convince her to come with me. I needed her as much as I needed my brothers. She was what would keep me sane when things with them got difficult – and I knew they would.

"You look amazing," I said as we stepped into the elevator.

She wore a simple pencil skirt and a fitted sweater, both in the same deep green that made her eyes stand out, but she couldn't have been more beautiful if she'd been in a designer gown.

"You're not so bad yourself," she replied with a smile.

I leaned down and gave her a soft kiss, my fingers brushing her cheek. "I missed you."

She looked surprised but pleased. "Me too." She laughed. "You're taking all the good lines."

We stepped into the lobby, hand-in-hand, then headed outside and down the sidewalk to where I'd parked. Once we were settled and I pulled away from the curb, she reached over and took my hand again.

"I was surprised you asked me to dinner," she said, her free fingers tracing patterns on the back of my hand. "You don't have to, you know."

"Don't have to what?"

"Take me to dinner. Don't get me wrong," she added quickly, "I'm happy to be here with you. I just don't want you to feel like I expect it. We were clear that this thing with us isn't a romantic relationship. You can ask me over for sex without all of this."

I glanced over at her, wondering if I should take the opening. "I wanted to spend time with you."

I could hear Jax in the back of my head telling me to man up.

She squeezed my hand. "I'd like that too."

When I'd done my research on romantic restaurants in Atlanta, Nikolai's Roof was near the top of the list, and I'd liked the look of the place. When Addison and I were seated at a small table near the windows, I knew I'd made the right choice. The view would've been great during the day, but at night, the city glowed.

"Atlanta is much more beautiful than I'd expected," Addison said after I placed a wine order.

Shit. Maybe this hadn't been the best place to go. I didn't want her falling in love with the city and not wanting to leave. I should have made a list of all the reasons why Boston was better than Atlanta. She was logical like me. She'd have appreciated that.

I didn't know how to do this.

"Are you okay?" She reached across the table and took my hand.

I nodded. I needed to find something to talk about. Anything.

"I called my brother this afternoon," I blurted out.

Dammit. That was going to lead straight to my question, but not in the way I'd wanted. This wasn't going the way I'd envisioned it at all.

"Which one?"

"Jax."

"That's great!" She shifted in her seat, her knees brushing against mine under the table. "How did it go?"

"Really well," I said. "Being engaged seems to agree with him."

"I'm happy for you." She squeezed my hand again, and something in her expression made me wonder if she wanted to say something more.

The waiter came back with our Merlot, and the conversation paused while he poured us each a glass. After thanking him, I took a healthy drink. It wasn't as intoxicating as hard liquor, but it was enough to relax me a bit.

"What did the two of you talk about?" Addison asked as she sipped her wine.

And here it went.

"He told me about Syll, and how being with her changed him." I reached for her hand this time, holding her fingers so that I could run my thumb over her knuckles.

"Love can do that, I suppose." Her gaze slid away from mine, and her smile seemed forced.

I took a deep breath. "I know it can," I agreed. "Because it's done that for me."

Her eyes snapped back to mine, wide and hopeful. "Cai?"

"When I asked you about us having a physical relationship, I was taking the easy way out." My fingers tightened around hers. "I've known I was in love with you from the moment you and Pansy came back from the field and you told me you'd been exposed. I didn't want to admit it, of course, but now, I can see it. The thought of losing you..." I shook my head. I couldn't think about it. "I should have told you then how I felt, especially after I realized that masked woman at the club was you. I'd been thinking about her – about *you* – constantly, and I should have seen it for what it was."

"Cai," she interrupted, her smile back to being genuine. "I think you're babbling."

A laugh burst out of me. She was right. I was babbling.

I needed to stop dancing around this and just say it.

I got up and walked around to where she was sitting,

crouching down so that we were closer to eye level. I took both of her hands in mine.

"I love you, Addison. And maybe it's not fair to tell you this way, but I don't want to lose you. I'm moving back to Boston to be closer to my brother, and I want you to come with me."

Her mouth fell open, and she stared at me.

"I'll understand if you say no, but I had to tell you before I put in my transfer request to the Boston office."

"You love me," she said quietly.

"I do."

"And you're moving back to Boston."

My heart gave a painful twist. "I am."

"But you want me to move back there too so we can be together."

I reached up and tucked a stray curl behind her ear. "Yes."

She gave me a long, searching look. "I thought you didn't do romantic relationships."

"So did I." I leaned forward and brushed my lips across hers. "But I think the truth was, I was really just waiting for you."

Her face lit up, and I knew what I'd said had addressed whatever doubts she'd been mulling over.

"If I can get my internship transferred to Boston, I'll go with you," she said.

"And if you can't?"

"I guess we'll have to try the long-distance thing."

Fuck that. I'd call in every favor owed to me if that's what it took. I'd worked my ass off my whole life, never settling for anything less than the best, and I'd be damned if I didn't do the same to ensure that Addison was by my side.

THIRTY-FOUR
CAI

"You really think he's in love?" I asked as I tried to figure out where I wanted to sit.

Being home again was...strange. Especially since not much had changed. The only concession I could see to Jax's presence was the abundance of electronics. Grandfather had always been old school. No gaming systems, no cell phones, no tablets. The only reason he'd conceded to a computer had been when he'd realized we needed one for school.

"I think he sounded exactly like you did when you called me about Addison," Jax said.

He bypassed the old leather chair that had always been Grandfather's and sat in a chair I didn't recognize. It fit with the décor but was newer. I finally settled at the near end of the couch, an eerie sense of déjà vu coming over me as I remembered sitting in this exact seat hundreds of times through my childhood and adolescence.

A short, curvy brunette waltzed into the room and leaned down to give Jax a brief kiss. "Your brother now thinks he's quite the expert on love."

He reached up and caught the back of her neck, pulling her back down for a deeper kiss that left her flushed and flustered.

"Tell Gilly I said that if she convinces you to buy more of that lingerie I like, she can buy herself some shoes on me."

Syll darted a look at me, embarrassment staining her cheeks red. "That's a dangerous bargain," she said. "You know how she loves her shoes."

Jax grinned, gripping his fiancée's hip possessively. "I do, but I love you in that lace and silk even more."

"I need to go," Syll said softly. She leaned forward and kissed him again. "And you need to talk to your brother."

It could have been an innocuous comment, stating the obvious, but something in her tone had me shifting in my seat. When Jax asked me to come over, I'd assumed he wanted to talk about my move, but now I wondered if there was something more behind it.

"It was nice to meet you, Cai," Syll said as she walked away. "I'm sure I'll be seeing you again soon."

"Good to meet you too," I said. As she disappeared, I turned back to Jax. "She's great."

He gave me an easy smile that I hadn't seen on his face since before our parents and sister died. I made a mental note to thank Syll for making this possible. If it hadn't been for her, I didn't doubt that Jax would've stayed the way he'd always been, hiring lawyers to try to get around Grandfather's stipulations rather than being willing to try to patch things between us.

"How did things go yesterday?" Jax asked, sipping his glass of scotch.

Highland Park, I assumed. It had been Grandfather's favorite.

"Really well," I answered. "Dr. Fenster isn't happy that I requested a transfer, but he talked to his contacts here and got things moving. He gave me a great recommendation too. The meeting went well. Dr. Harmon said he'd give me the official confirmation by Monday afternoon, but unofficially, the transfer has gone through."

"That's great," Jax said sincerely. "And Addison?"

Just the mention of her was enough to make me smile. "She's coming with me. I hadn't been certain I could get her internship transferred, but once I explained how her thesis and my own work were closely related, Dr. Harmon agreed to make room for her up here."

"I look forward to meeting her," Jax said.

"I think she and Syll are going to get along. They'll bond over having to take care of us."

He laughed and nodded. "That sounds about right." He took another drink from his glass. "If you need any help finding a place, let me know."

"Thanks. I'll do that." Then I added, "I'm just glad my lease is up at the end of the month."

"What about your girl?" he asked. "Are you two looking for separate places, or together?"

I held my glass between both hands and stared down into the amber liquid. "I want to ask her to live with me," I admitted, "but I think it's too fast."

"Cai, you're talking to the man who proposed to a woman after knowing her for a month. And most of that month, she was pissed at me."

My mouth lifted in a partial smile. "Good point."

"Do you know where you're going to stay if you don't have a place before you start work up here?" he asked. "Because you're both welcome to stay here. I've cleaned out most of Grandfather's things from the floor he used. It has its own private entrance, and we put in a kitchenette in one of the rooms."

I swallowed hard, touched by the surprising offer. "Thank you. I'll probably take you up on that."

Jax drained his glass, his expression becoming serious. This was it, my gut told me, the real reason he asked me to stop by before I returned to Atlanta. He stood and walked over to the curio in the corner. He took something out of the middle drawer and brought it over to me.

"I received this in the mail three weeks ago." He returned to his seat.

I recognized the handwriting, and my heart gave a painful squeeze. Grandfather had left Jax a letter. Why, then, hadn't I gotten one?

I took the letter out of the envelope and began to read, hoping for an answer to my question.

Jax,

Upon the event of my death...

The longer I read, the more I wished this was some awful joke. But I knew that neither Jax nor Grandfather had that sort of sense of humor. When I finished it, I slumped back in the chair and looked up at my brother.

"What the hell?"

Jax nodded, his expression grim. "That was pretty much my reaction too."

"He hired a PI because he thought the car accident wasn't an accident." I felt like I needed to repeat it, as if it would make a difference.

"Bartholomew Constantine," Jax said. "I've talked to him."

I had hundreds of questions, and the one that popped out surprised me. "It's been twenty-four years. He's still around?"

"He'd just opened his business when Grandfather hired him," Jax explained. "He's in his fifties now, and he's got a thriving practice. Nothing dicey in his past, nearly one hundred percent client satisfaction, and the few complaints I could find seemed like petty things."

"I don't see what that has to do with Grandfather's suspicions," I said. "He clearly didn't find enough evidence to convince Grandfather that he was wrong."

Jax was silent for a moment, his hands clasped in front of him, his posture tense. His eyes met mine, and they burned with an intensity I hadn't seen in a long time.

"The thing is, Cai, after talking to Constantine, I don't think Grandfather was wrong at all. I think someone killed our family."

THIRTY-FIVE
ADDISON

IF SOMEONE HAD TOLD ME TWO MONTHS AGO THAT BY MID-March, I'd be in Boston with Dr. Cai Hunter, who was not only my supervisor but also my lover, and that we'd moved to allow him to reconcile with his billionaire brother...just thinking about how insane that sounded made my head hurt.

I wondered how long it would take me to get used to the surreal world that was now my life. When Cai had asked me to go with him to Boston, all my common sense told me that saying yes would be the stupidest decision I'd ever make, but I hadn't listened, because what I felt for Cai defied common sense.

I'd spent a few days with my stomach in knots while Cai worked things out for not only his transfer but mine – as well as telling his soon-to-be new bosses about our relationship. But one thing I'd learned about Cai was that when he had his mind set on something, no one could stop him.

The fact that we were here, with our new jobs officially starting Monday morning and our relationship out in the open, was a testament to his persistence.

We'd just said goodnight to Jax and Syll after a wonderful dinner, and were now on 'our' floor, which was larger than both my apartment in Atlanta and the apartment where I'd been raised in Minnesota. I couldn't imagine having grown up in this house, with so much room, even with having three siblings. Cai said not much had changed, except on this floor, a kitchenette, and a door had been added to make it more like a separate apartment. It made it a little less awkward to share the house with Jax and Syll.

"Everything all right with Dorly?" Cai asked as he toed off his shoes. "I'm guessing that's who texted you during dinner."

"She's fine," I said as I took off my shoes and stretched my arms above my head. My joints popped pleasantly. "Just freaking out about Codie moving in tomorrow."

"Didn't Codie stay at the apartment most nights anyway?"

I nodded. "Dorly said she's glad me leaving gave her the kick in the ass she needed to finally ask Codie to move in, but she's nervous. She's never lived with anyone before. Roommates, yeah, but not with someone she loved."

Cai turned toward me, and the heat in his eyes kicked my pulse up a notch. We'd gotten here yesterday, but with everything we'd been doing, we hadn't done anything more than kiss or exchange innocent touches like holding hands. One would think after having gone most off my life without sex, it'd be easy to go a few days.

Not so much.

"Go stand by the balcony doors."

I did as I was told, turning away from him when he twirled his finger, giving me a silent command. I watched his reflection in the glass, my heart skipping and tripping as anticipation danced across my nerves. It was times like this I wondered if this was how it felt to be an addict craving a fix.

"Spread your legs."

He stood behind me, the heat from his body flowing over my skin, enveloping me. He unzipped my dress, easing it off my body with a slow, sensual caress. It dropped to the floor, and I kicked it aside without taking my eyes off his reflection.

He didn't say a word as he reached down between my legs and moved my panties to one side. I gasped as he slid a finger inside me, twisting and curling it until it rubbed my g-spot.

"Ahh..." A shaky breath escaped.

"Do you like that, Little Red?"

"Yes, yes, yes..."

He added a second finger, pumping them both into me hard and fast. I swayed forward and put out my hands, catching myself on the glass.

"What do you want?" His voice was a quiet rumble, full of the promise of sex. "Tell me."

"I want to come," I said immediately.

"What do you want me to do to you?" he clarified.

"Make me come," I said. "Fingers, mouth, cock, I don't care. I need to come so badly. I need you to take me out of my head, make me forget about everything else. I just want to think about you and how you make me feel and not have to worry about work or finding a place to live or..."

My run of words disappeared into a yelp as Cai sunk his teeth into my ass. He hadn't broken skin, but he hadn't been gentle either. It was exactly what I needed though. The shock of it jerked me out of my head and took me to that lovely place where I didn't have to think or plan but could simply let go and give Cai control over all of me.

I cried out as a finger invaded my ass, the burn sudden, providing the spark I needed to reach my first climax of the night. He worked both of his hands, using those long, skilled fingers of his to push me from one orgasm into a second without pause.

When he finally removed his fingers, my knees buckled. He caught me around the waist and swung me up into his arms. He carried me into the bedroom we'd claimed and laid me on the bed. My body was still limp as he rolled me onto my side and pulled my knees up to my chest.

I was vaguely aware of him removing his clothes, but it wasn't until I felt the tip of his cock nudging at my pussy that I completely came back to the present. He leaned over me, one arm under my knees to keep my body folded in half, and he nipped my earlobe.

"We're going to work that ass open soon, Little Red," he promised.

Before I could respond, he snapped his hips forward, sending my muscles into convulsions as they struggled to adapt to a position they didn't understand. I started to wail, but Cai's hand quickly covered my mouth.

"Shh, Little Red. Don't want Jax and Syll running up here, thinking you're in trouble."

As he drove into me, his body colliding with mine over and over, I didn't care about Jax and Syll. In fact, I was confident that if they did see us, they'd completely understand why I was making those sounds. This position made me tighter than usual, and Cai was far from small. Still, I wouldn't trade the pain-edged pleasure for anything.

Time melted away, and all I knew was the feel of sweat-slicked skin slipping and muscles straining and oh my fucking –

"Cai!!" I screamed against his hand as my vision went white.

"Not yet," he said through gritted teeth.

I could feel the tension in him, everything taut and ready to snap, but he didn't falter. He was in perfect control as he sent me from brilliant light to a graying darkness, my brain shutting down as it found itself incapable of processing anything more.

When I came to, I was still curled on my side, and he was softening inside me. His cock slipped out as he lay down behind me, wrapping his body around mine. I kissed his arm, too exhausted to reach anything else.

"I love you," he said as he smoothed curls back from my face.

"I love you too."

I'd never imagined saying those words or having them said back to me, but now I couldn't imagine living without them. Not for the sake of the words alone, but because of who said them.

"You know," he said slowly, "I've been thinking. It doesn't make sense for us to try to find two different places to live."

I turned my head, so I could see his face. "What are you saying, Cai?"

He rested his forehead on mine. "I want to fall asleep like this and wake up together. I want us to eat our meals and go to work together."

I tried not to feel too much hope. "I think I'm going to need you to spell this out so there's no misunderstanding."

"I want you to move in with me," he said without any hesitation. "Or, more accurately, I want us to find a place together. I know it's fast, but you've seen Jax and Syll, and they're engaged after just one month. You and I are just as well-matched as they are, if not better. We've shared space before, plus we do it at work too."

This was crazy, but so was every other part of our lives that had brought us together. It was that, as much as anything else, that made me smile. "Yes."

"Yes?" His face lit up with a huge smile.

I nodded, rolling over so that we were facing each other. I pressed my mouth to his, a quick, heated kiss. "Yes, Cai. I want to live with you. I don't care what anyone else thinks. We belong together."

He slid his hands down to grasp my ass and yank me tight against him. "Damn right we do."

Our decision didn't mean everything would magically work itself out, or that the tension between the brothers would resolve itself, but it did mean that we wouldn't be facing any of it alone, and that was more than good enough for me.

THE END

The Hunter Brothers continues in Slade's story,
His Hunger.

ALSO BY M. S. PARKER

His Obsession

His Control

His Hunger

Big O's

Rescued by the Woodsman

Sex Coach

The Billionaire's Muse

Bound

One Night Only

Damage Control

Take Me, Sir

Make Me Yours

The Billionaire's Sub

The Billionaire's Mistress

Con Man Box Set

HERO Box Set

A Legal Affair Box Set

The Client

Indecent Encounter

Dom X Box Set

Unlawful Attraction Box Set

Chasing Perfection Box Set

Blindfold Box Set

Club Prive Box Set

The Pleasure Series Box Set

Exotic Desires Box Set

Pure Lust Box Set

Casual Encounter Box Set

Sinful Desires Box Set

Twisted Affair Box Set

Serving HIM Box Set

ABOUT THE AUTHOR

M. S. Parker is a USA Today Bestselling author and the author of over fifty spicy romance series and novels.

Living part-time in Las Vegas, part-time on Maui, she enjoys sitting by the pool with her laptop writing her next spicy romance.

Growing up all she wanted to be was a dancer, actor and author. So far only the latter has come true but M. S. Parker hasn't retired her dancing shoes just yet. She is still waiting for the call to appear on Dancing With The Stars.

When M. S. isn't writing, she can usually be found reading–oops, scratch that! She is always writing.

For more information:
www.msparker.com
msparkerbooks@gmail.com

ACKNOWLEDGMENTS

First, I would like to thank all of my readers. Without you, my books would not exist. I truly appreciate each and every one of you.

A big THANK YOU goes out to all the Facebook fans, street team, beta readers, and advanced reviewers. You are a HUGE part of the success of all my series.

Also thank you to my editor Lynette, my proofreader Nancy, and my wonderful cover designer, Sinisa. You make my ideas and writing look so good.